Morgan leveled her pistol at him. . . .

"That seems extreme," Shaw said.

"Get down!" she said.

He ducked—and she fired. She saw a redcoat fall from his horse. That was one down—how many more to go? Too many, she thought.

She tossed the pistol to Shaw, along with her powder flask and bullet pouch. He stared at them blankly for a second.

"Reload!" she ordered.

"It's hard to imagine what part of your life would require me to speak Latin—" he began.

Morgan bellowed, "Reload, damn your eyes, or I'll choke you where you sit!"

Based on the major motion picture from Carolco Pictures.

Cutthroat Island

A novel by John Gregory Betancourt
Based on a screenplay by Robert King and Marc Norman
and a story by Michael Frost Beckner & James Gorman
and Bruce A. Evans & Raynold Gideon

A TOM DOHERTY ASSOCIATES BOOK
NEW YORK

This is a work of fiction. All the characters and events portrayed in this book are fictitious, and any resemblance to real people or events is purely coincidental.

CUTTHROAT ISLAND

A Forge Book
Published by Tom Doherty Associates, Inc.
175 Fifth Avenue
New York, NY 10010

Forge® is a registered trademark of Tom Doherty Associates, Inc.

ISBN: 0-812-54304-1

First edition: December 1995

Printed in the United States of America

0 9 8 7 6 5 4 3 2 1

This book is for Greg Cox, with thanks.

1

Tortuga Cove: 1688

T wilight brought a warm southern breeze scented with brine and tropical flowers to the pirate ship christened the *Reaper*. Waves lapped softly at the ship's hull, and the cries of distant gulls from the island of Tortuga could be heard in the distance.

Tonight Black Harry Adams was going to die. That was the one thought in his mind. *I'm going to die.*

His wooden leg slipped out from under him again and again. The ropes binding his wrists dug painfully into his flesh. His back and arms ached from open, bleeding wounds where he'd been cruelly whipped by chains.

Then he heard mocking laughter, and a sudden chill went down his spine. He knew that voice only too well. It belonged to his bastard half-brother, Douglas Brown, a quietly vicious and very clever man who deserved his nickname, "Dawg."

Black Harry heard a familiar loud crack of wood striking wood and knew a gangplank had been slammed into place. He swallowed. He felt rough hands tying something to his one good foot. He didn't have to be able to see to know it was an anchor.

His brother, seated in the shadows, focused a burning, angry gaze upon him. Dawg Brown slowly leaned forward, a faint mocking smile on his lips.

"Now, Mr. Snelgrave," Dawg said.

Snelgrave, a foul-smelling and fouler-looking cutthroat, with scars from dozens of battles and a crooked nose, slowly smiled. Two of his front teeth were gone. He raised a cutlass in his good hand—his other hand was just a tarred stump with a length of chain attached— and prodded Harry none too gently toward the end of the plank.

Black Harry solemnly acquiesced. He knew there was no use protesting.

Dawg sliced off a hunk of salt pork, stabbed it with a dagger, and brought it up to his mouth. He took a large bite.

"All the way to the edge, Harry," Dawg

called as he chewed. Harry knew his brother was enjoying this situation to its fullest. "Feel it with your toes. You've dropped enough anchors—you know how they fall."

Harry gritted his teeth. If he had to die, it would be with dignity. "Eat shit, brother," he snarled back. "I'll give you the fork."

"You'll hold your breath as you sink," Dawg said softly, leaning forward, a gleam in his eye. "Then at some point, you'll think, It's no use, there's no hope. Then you'll scream and the sea will rush in . . ."

"I always knew I'd die in the ocean," Harry said, "so God rot you, Dawg."

Snelgrave prodded him again with the cutlass. Dawg Brown began to laugh. And Black Harry Adams felt true fear for what was to come.

Glasspoole reined in his horse at the villa's back wall. He was a tall, dark-skinned man astride an equally black horse, and he knew he didn't have a second to waste. He'd been searching the island all day and he'd about run out of places to look. If Morgan wasn't here, then luck had truly run out for his captain, Black Harry Adams.

His mount shied a bit to the side, but steadied when he pulled back the reins. He glanced over at young Bowen, also mounted, then back at the third horse they'd brought. This had better be the place, he thought.

"Morgan!" he shouted in his booming Caribbean accent. "Morgan! Where are you?"

Morgan Adams, Black Harry Adams's strapping, fiery pirate daughter, stuck her head out from a second-floor window. Glasspoole felt a wave of relief rush through him. Morgan's long, curled black tresses cascaded around her head, and her full red lips parted a bit questioningly as she stared down at him. She appeared to be wrapped in a sheet and not much else.

"What is it, Mr. Glasspoole?" she called down. "I'm busy at the moment."

Bowen called, "Mr. Blair's compliments— Dawg has captured your father!"

"Damn him!" Morgan ducked back inside. "Wait for me!" Glasspoole heard her shout.

Glasspoole leaned back in his saddle and exchanged a quick glance with Bowen.

"She'll be right down," Glasspoole said. "Pray heaven it's in time."

Inside the villa, Morgan began a frantic search for her clothes. She barely glanced at the handsome, naked, and all too aristocratic Portuguese lieutenant whose company she had been enjoying for the afternoon. She had hoped to continue their dalliance well into the night, but it seemed fate was against their liaison in more ways than one.

"Is something wrong?" he asked mildly, pulling the sheet a bit higher. "You are going so soon?"

"Where are my pants?" she demanded.

"Tangled with the bedclothes, I believe." He gestured toward the foot of the bed with his chin. "I can just see your buckle—yes, there."

Morgan dragged out her pants and pulled them on quickly, then shrugged on her shirt. She left it unlaced while she strapped on her cutlass.

"But I thought you and I were forever," the lieutenant said, an edge creeping into his voice. "I want you so badly . . ."

Morgan scarcely heard. She lifted the bedclothes once more. "Where's my dagger . . . ?" she muttered. She glanced around the room, then over at the lieutenant—and found herself staring down the muzzle of his pistol.

She sighed. "I really don't have time for this now," she said.

"I want you so badly," said the lieutenant, standing, "but then so does the governor of Port Royal, who will pay well for the capture of Morgan Adams, the pirate!"

"You knew who I was?" Morgan asked. She sat on the bed as though he were holding a flower toward her instead of a pistol. Calmly she began pulling on her boots.

"All the time," the lieutenant said. "You are not without a certain . . . *notoriety*, Morgan. I thought it would be more amusing if I took my pleasure first."

"You are heartless, Lieutenant."

"My apologies, senorita!"

"But you're right. I found it more amusing this way also, since I knew you knew."

"What!" The lieutenant glanced at the door as if half expecting it to come crashing down and her pirate friends to come rushing in to her rescue.

Morgan merely pointed at the pistol. "By the way, that won't work. I took these." She opened her hand, revealing the pistol balls.

Dressed now, she whistled sharply—and her pet monkey, King Charles, leaped onto her shoulder. She idly stroked his head for a second, then strode toward the doorway. The lieutenant backed furiously away, as if her slightest touch might kill him. Morgan snorted inwardly. What fools these young naval officers were. It was little wonder pirated ruled the Caribbean these days.

In the doorway, she paused and looked back. She had enjoyed this one. He had been good in bed, and he was rather attractive. In other times and under other circumstances, she would happily have seen him again.

"I promise to write," she said, and then she blew him a kiss. Let him tell his comrades this story, she thought. She all but waltzed out the door.

* * *

Five minutes later Morgan felt sweat starting to pour down her back. Beneath her, the gray mare Glasspoole had brought strained as it ran, sweat already flecking her hide. Parrots and lovebirds called protests as they crashed past; tiny monkeys like King Charles chittered in the treetops.

Never before had this path seemed so long, she thought. It twisted and turned, doubling back on itself several times, and each time it did she cursed anew the delay. Hanging vines clutched at her face and arms. She had to keep constant watch in the growing twilight for any jutting roots and fallen trees that might trip her mare. The last thing she needed right now was a horse with a broken leg.

Dawg had her father. That was all Glasspoole needed to say to get her moving. The thought chilled her to her soul. She loathed her uncle and would gladly have slit his throat given the chance. And not just for what he'd done to her father, but for what he'd done to her so long ago.

She forced her thoughts away from that dark place. One thing at a time. She'd have her revenge on Uncle Douglas, but only when *she* was ready.

They burst from the jungle into a clearing, and for the first time the other two caught up with her and rode alongside. Her mare was trembling with exhaustion and rolling her eyes; she let her slow to a trot.

"What happened?" she called to Glasspoole. "I want to know!"

"Your father sent for you two days ago—" he began.

"I was coming—"

"He did not know this," Glasspoole said.

Bowen added, "And that's when Dawg grabbed him. Lord knows what he's doing with him . . ."

She pulled King Charles from her shoulder and tossed him to Bowen, then spurred her horse. The gray mare leapt forward, sand crunching under her hooves.

Near darkness had fallen by the time she made it to the gently rolling surf, but she didn't stop at the sea. She rode out until the horse was waist-deep, which brought her close enough to the jolly boat.

She leapt from her horse, tumbling the lone pirate working on the oars onto his back. Before he could draw his pistol, she clobbered him with a bailing bucket.

She paused a second, stilling her breathing, straining to hear any sounds of alarm from the *Reaper*. Her heartbeat pounded in her ears, but no other sounds except the murmur of surf reached her. The celebration continued aboard the *Reaper*; nobody had spotted her attack.

She rolled the pirate's limp body overboard— let the deep have him, she thought, and good riddance—and continued fitting the oars into their locks.

Clamping them in place, she sat with her back to the pirate ship and began to pull with all her might. Ashore, Glasspoole and Bowen retrieved her mare's reins and paused to watch her progress. The deepening twilight made them indistinct shapes that soon disappeared altogether in the distance.

The taunting and poking with the cutlass seemed to drag on forever, Black Harry Adams thought, but since the alternative—dropping off the plank with an anchor tied to his one good foot—seemed infinitely worse, he made little objection.

Suddenly Dawg reached into a leather pouch around his neck and removed a yellowed bit of paper. It was old and fragile, Harry knew, and he knew as well exactly what it was: a torn corner of a treasure map.

"I got this off our brother Richard last week," Dawg said, holding it up for Harry to see. "Not willingly—that's his blood on the borders. With your piece, all I'll need is Mordechai's . . ."

Harry snorted. "Your luck's run out, then, Dawg. I don't have it."

"No? Where else might it be, then? With your Morgan, perhaps?"

"Her?" Harry forced a laugh. "She blows with the wind—I ain't seen her in months."

Dawg said, very softly, "I think you lie,

Harry. How is the little thing—still vexed I put my hands on her when she was small?"

"All right," Harry said suddenly. He knew he had to play for time until he could think of something or Dawg *would* hunt down his daughter. "I hid it," he went on. "I knew you'd come."

"Progress," Dawg said. "Where is it?"

"Up here," Harry said, pointing to his head.

"Your head?" Dawg said. "Well, I will have access to that. Come back aboard, dear brother—I will open it up. Mr. Snelgrave?"

Grinning evilly, Snelgrave started out on the gangplank after Harry.

"You won't get the pleasure, Dawg. I'll see you in hell before you get that map!"

Taking a deep breath—though he knew it would do him little good in the end—he leapt off the gangplank.

It was a mere second's fall to the water, but in that time he glimpsed a small boat and his daughter Morgan's startled face. Then he hit with a splash and cool dark water rushed over him.

Hands grabbed him—it *was* Morgan, he realized. She was leaning out and holding him from a small boat.

Above them, Dawg Brown leaned over the rail, straining to see the small jollyboat in the water next to his ship.

"Who was that, now?" he demanded.

Beside him, Snelgrave said, "Looked to me like the girl." He turned away, suddenly bellowing, "Lower the cutter—find them!"

Black Harry saw his daughter struggling to reach the dagger in her boot, but she needed both hands to hold him up against the weight of the anchor.

"Leave me!" Harry whispered to his daughter.

"Shut up and help me!" she whispered back.

Somehow she got under him and heaved with all her might. Harry grabbed the gunwales. He managed to hold himself there against the terrible downward drag on his leg. Then his eyes went wide. With a creaking of pulleys, the *Reaper*'s crew began to lower the cutter over the side of the ship—right on top of him!

Suddenly gunshots rang out and balls *thock*ed the water around them. He felt something strike him like a punch in the chest and gasped in sudden pain.

"Stop firing!" Dawg screamed. Harry looked up and saw him knocking muskets from the hands of his crew. "That would only make sense if I had the map! Mr. Snelgrave . . . ?"

Snelgrave began barking orders.

Harry couldn't hold himself up any longer, and as he released his grip, the rotting timbers of the jollyboat also gave way. The rope around his foot continued to pull him down, and Morgan—still clutching him—was yanked overboard and into the water.

Harry felt his arms go weak. He couldn't keep his grip on the gunwales. He let go and plunged deep into the sea, toward the sandy floor and hell itself.

2

Morgan clung tightly to her father's limp body as they sank. The dagger she'd pulled from her boot was razor sharp; she knew she only needed few more seconds to free her father.

He didn't seem to want her help, though. He pushed her away, grabbing the dagger from her hand.

Suddenly she saw the dark blood from his wound clouding the water and understood. He thought he was already close to dead from his wound and wanted her to get away while she still could. Gritting her teeth, she forced the dagger from his hand and closed her fist more firmly around it. Already the pressure from the depth made her ears ache; she longed desperately to breathe but knew she couldn't. Two lives depended on it.

Pulling herself down along his body to his ankle, once more she began to saw at the rope. The strands parted reluctantly. She began to let the air trickle from her mouth.

Her father seemed to lose consciousness. He floated limply, a rag doll tethered to an anchor. Hurry, Morgan told herself. There's not much time left.

Finally, when her lungs were bursting, the rope parted. She returned her dagger to its sheath as the anchor plunged away into the darkness below. Grasping her father around the waist, she swam up diagonally, trying to surface as far from the *Reaper* as quickly as she could.

She broke water, gasping softly. It took all her strength to get her father's head above the water. Blinking her eyes, it took her a moment to get her bearings.

On the other side of Dawg's ship . . . and safe, at least for the moment. She could hear Snelgrave bellowing orders.

Still holding her father's head up, Morgan began to swim a little unsteadily toward the shore. Sooner or later one of the boats would come around the *Reaper*, she knew, and it wouldn't take long for those manning it to spot her. She had to get ashore as quickly as possible. Glasspoole and Bowen would be waiting. They'd help her get her father to safety.

After what seemed an eternity, Morgan reached a small cave. She found she could stand and half carried, half dragged her father up out of the water and onto a small ledge. She leaned over him and grasped his hand in hers. His eyes were open; his breath came in rasps. At least he was still alive, she thought. Several times she'd feared he'd died in the water, only to hear him take another breath a few seconds later.

"What . . ." Black Harry said. He began to cough.

"Lie still, Father," she said.

"What have I done in my life to get you?" he whispered.

"Father, I'm sorry," she said.

She still had her dagger. She pulled it from her boot sheath and slit his clothes to expose the wound. It was round and puckered, still oozing blood. In the moonlight, it looked bad, but somehow Morgan knew it would look ten times worse come morning.

"Wasting yourself . . . boozing . . . carousing . . ." Every word seemed an agony to him. Morgan felt her insides knotting up at his words. "Shameful, childish . . . not worthy . . . look what you've done . . ."

Morgan found her hands were trembling. "Dawg will pay for this. I swear—"

"You leave Dawg alone!"

"I'll fly his bloody head as my banner—"

"You'll leave Dawg well to leeward!" Her father seemed to draw on an inner reserve of strength. He raised his head and looked her in the eyes. "There'll come a time for Dawg later—when you grow up, after you find your Uncle Mordechai and take my men, make my men yours. They don't at the moment look up to you, Morgan. Understandably. You have a lot to learn."

"I'll get you back to your ship," she said.

"I'll not see the *Morning Star* again," he said. "She's yours now—God help us all."

"No, Father!" Morgan cried. "Don't say that!"

"Sharpen your knife," he said.

"No—the ball's in too deep—"

He lay back again. "I want you to shave my head."

"What?" she exclaimed.

"Morgan, for once in your life, do as I tell you!"

Morgan nodded; he must have a reason for it, she thought. Her father always had a reason for everything he did. She ran the blade a couple of times against the stone ledge, treating it like a whetstone, then tested it with her thumb. It was as sharp as ever. Leaning forward, she pulled a strand of her father's hair taut and cut it away.

As she worked, her father said, "In 1619 the cargo ship *Santa Susanna* was taken by the *Sea Devil*, a pirate cutter out of Ocrocoke. In the hold, they found the richest cargo ever to leave the Americas . . . four million pounds of Spanish plunder."

Morgan looked around for something to pillow her father's head and found some seaweed, which she arranged as comfortably as she could. Now that his hair was short enough, she scraped the blade's edge against his skull like a razor, shaving him bald.

After a long pause, her father went on. "The *Sea Devil* set course for Tortuga, but . . . a great gale caught her and she wrecked on an island. Cutthroat Island."

Morgan paused. Cutthroat Island? She'd read maps since she was just out of nappies, and not once had she heard of the place. For a second she wondered if it might be some delusion, but the intense look in her father's eyes drove that thought from her. If he said it was real, real it was.

"It's on no maps—nor in any logs," he said, as if reading her mind. "No man's survived the island, save one—your grandfather, Fingers Adams." He drew a deep breath. "On his deathbed he made a map, tore it into three, sent a piece to each of his sons. We were no great friends in life, and we each got a third of the map, one showing the parallel, another the longitude, the last the treasure itself. No piece for Dawg, being Fingers's bastard. And being the bastard he is, he's killing us and grabbing it all. Do you see it yet . . . ?"

He leaned his head forward. In the glow of

the moonlight, Morgan could see a faint line tattooed across her father's scalp.

"What is it?" she breathed.

"My third of the map. Your uncle Mordechai waits for me with his at Spittalfield Tavern. Take the *Morning Star* as captain. The men will serve you if you search for gold, and if you find it they'll respect you. If you don't they might slit your throat. You'll have to take the map with you."

"No, no," Morgan said.

"I told you . . . you'd have to grow up . . ."

"You ask too much of me," Morgan said.

"You can do it!" he said. "You were born to it—you lived your whole life on a holystoned deck! It's always been cakes and ale with you, sweet Morgan. But you'll have no time for that now. And I'll never know how you've done . . . will I . . . ?"

He took a last deep breath and abruptly grew still. His gaze stared off to the horizon . . . a horizon he would never see again.

Morgan closed his eyes, then kissed him tenderly. If only she'd come more quickly. If only she'd been a better daughter. If only she had it all to do over again.

She turned him around. Moonlight reflected off the water onto his head. For the first time she could see it all clearly: a map tattooed on his scalp, showing part of an island, with Latin words over it.

"I loved you," she whispered, cradling his head in her lap. "I'm so, so sorry, Father."

She sat there for most of the night, listening to the waves, listening to the wind, listening to the searchers from Dawg's ship. But mostly she listened to her heart.

When at last she rose, it was with a new determination. She would do all her father had asked. And later, when she'd won that golden Spanish treasure, she'd take care of Dawg. She had another, even older score to settle, and she vowed that whatever might come of it, she'd see him dead.

3

Port Royal, Jamaica

Lord Ainslee, governor of Jamaica, raised an eyeglass to one eye and peered around the ballroom with an expression of supreme indifference. Sixty dancers swirled around the dance floor to the accompaniment of a spritely minuet: beautiful petticoated women and handsome periwigged men, all dressed in their finest clothes and bedecked with their most dazzling jewels, all come to his home for the annual Governor's Ball.

He had invited them all: English, French, Spanish, and Dutch alike, anyone and everyone of significance in Port Royal. So far from home, he found politics less important than good company. Port Royal had few enough true bluebloods that he had to invite anyone of any note lest the festivities turn out little larger than a good-sized dinner party.

He noticed young Mandy Ricketts standing to one side of the dance floor, fanning herself slowly and watching the dancers with a forlorn expression. Her gown was a gorgeous concoction of French lace and Chinese silk and easily set the others in the room to shame, and yet no man had asked her for even one dance as far as he could tell. It was her looks. If Helen's face had launched a thousand ships, Mandy Ricketts's would have sent them back to port: a severe overbite, large nose, and angular— one might say bony—body that not even the most expensive of gowns could hide. At least the way she did her hair concealed ears that jutted out from her head, almost like sails on a ship.

Ainslee sighed. Miss Ricketts's father brought a lot of money to Jamaica; he would have to see that she enjoyed herself this night. The steady growth of his own fortune might well depend upon her reaction to his ball tonight.

Governor Ainslee did not change expression as he considered all the possibilities; he had worked long and hard to achieve an exceptional look: cool, aloof, superior. It masked a cunning intellect and a mind racing to consider every option and alternative. Now, he thought, of all the bachelors present, who

could he most successfully pair with Miss
Ricketts for the evening?

Ah, there was just the fellow: young, Lieutenant Trotter, and in his red dress uniform
with the gold piping at sleeve and collar, he
cut quite a striking figure. The fact that he
was an officer would, no doubt, impress Miss
Ricketts all the more. Although Trotter had
served in Port Royal's town redcoat regiment
for several years with little distinction, he
would have a score of amusing little stories to
tell. These waters swarmed with pirates and
their ilk, and if he exaggerated his importance
to impress a girl . . . what army officer didn't?
Yes, Trotter would do quite nicely, Ainslee
thought.

He cut smoothly through the crowd, nodding
to people as he passed, maintaining his
friendly yet oh-so-superior expression. It was a
governor's duty to stand above those he gov-
erned, he told himself. Though seemingly pur-
poseless to the casual observer, his course took
him to the refreshment table soon enough,
where he stopped beside Lieutenant Trotter
and lowered his voice.

"Mandy Ricketts stands there alone." He
made a subtle motion toward the side of the
room where Miss Ricketts stood watching
the dancers. "Her father brings a fortune in
investments to our little island. It wouldn't do
to have her complain about our society. Dance
with her."

Trotter gave her a quick glance. "She's powerful homely."

"That may be—but grit your teeth and do it, Mr. Trotter." He paused and caught Trotter's arm before the young lieutenant could obey. "Never mind. You've missed your opportunity, Mr. Trotter. Another man takes the plunge . . ."

Trotter relaxed noticeably.

"Now, now, she wasn't as bad as all that."

"Truly, sir, I had my eye on another . . ."

"Good, good. Keep up the good work." Ainslee patted him on the shoulder and continued his circuit of the room. Every so often his gaze drifted back to Mandy Ricketts, and each time he wondered what a man like William Shaw could possibly want with her.

Mandy Ricketts felt her heart fluttering and, for a second, could barely keep track of what the young man was saying.

"There's every reason why I should be alone tonight, being a stranger here, but a woman with grace such as yours should never be untended. May I have the honor of this dance?"

He offered her his arm, and she accepted.

As he swept her out onto the dance floor, he said, "My name's William Shaw, but my friends call me Bill. And you, ma'am?"

"Amanda—Lady Ricketts. You've heard of my father, surely. Are you at leisure, Mr. Shaw, or do you follow a profession?"

"A most serious one, ma'am. I am a medical man—a doctor."

"Oh, my!" Mandy said.

"I studied at Leyden, then higher anatomy for a year with Dreyfuss at Leipzig."

This was all too good to be true, Mandy thought. He twirled her, then touched her hair—almost an embrace! she thought giddily. They danced on.

"With higher anatomy," she said, trying to sound as provocative as some of the older girls at boarding school used to be, "you must know a great deal about the human body."

"Indeed, ma'am," Shaw said. "Every bit of it. All the ins and outs, you might say."

"Oooh," Mandy said, blushing.

"Yes, ma'am," Shaw said, entirely straight-faced. "In medicine, it's our obligation to probe to the very bottom of things."

They met, twirled, and this time his hand lingered behind her head. He bent to whisper in her ear, "We must, in fact, explode ancient superstitions—shake truths violently from the body—"

Mandy, almost swooning, dipped with him. The dance ended; after brief applause, he escorted her to her seat. Many fanned herself, feeling hot and flushed. She'd never met anyone like Dr. William Shaw before. She turned a new phrase over in her mind: *Mrs. William Shaw* . . . and she liked the sound it made.

* * *

The man calling himself Dr. William Shaw plastered a smile on his face as he cut through the crowds heading toward the refreshment table. He could feel the weight of Mandy Ricketts's diamond comb safely in his coat pocket, the plum prize for the evening, better than everything else he'd been able to pocket. She had been a silly girl, an easy target, and he almost felt sorry for how easily she had been duped. Still, he had to make his living, and doctoring paid nowhere as well as theft these days.

"You, sir!" someone called behind him.

He quickened his pace and pretended not to hear. A nervous prickling ran up and down his arms and neck. He'd been so careful—had someone seen him?

A young army officer, a lieutenant he saw from the insignia on the man's sleeves, suddenly blocked his way. He drew up short and tried to stare the man down. That's what he always did when things got tight: brazened them out.

"Forgive my rudeness," the lieutenant said. "Trotter's the name—I'm with the regiment. I make it a habit to know everyone who visits here, and I find I've yet to make your acquaintance."

"William Shaw, sir," he said, somewhat archly. "Dr. Shaw, in fact."

"Most happy." Trotter gave him a slight bow.

"If I may ask, what ship did you come in on, Doctor? The Bristol packet?"

"I believe that was it—I may not have the name right. I'm all at sea when it comes to things nautical."

"The reason I asked," Trotter said, "was that the Bristol packet doesn't arrive until a week from Wednesday."

"Yes?" He shifted uneasily. "Then I must have gotten the name wrong. If you'll excuse me, sir, I have a patient waiting."

Far off, he heard a woman's piercing, frantic voice—Mandy Ricketts's voice, he thought—rising above the murmur of talk: "That's him!" she was saying. "That man lifted my diamond comb!"

Like dominoes, other voices began to join in as all the women present checked their valuables: "My emerald brooch!" another woman cried. "My pearl dangles!" cried a third.

He stepped to the side, but Trotter blocked his way. He felt the floor drop out from under him. Smiling a bit, he shrugged, then stepped hard on the lieutenant's toe as Trotter made a quick grab for him.

No brazening this out, he thought, running for his life.

"Sergeant of the Guard!" he heard Lieutenant Trotter shout. "To arms! To arms!"

The doorway seemed the most obvious way out, but as he approached, two redcoats blocked his access to it. He pushed through a crowd of gaily dressed women, ignoring their indignant protests, and spotted the grand staircase leading down to the governor's mansion's lower floor.

He dashed toward it, only to find his way blocked by a crowd of ladies, who began to shriek. Cursing, he leapt onto the marble railing beside them and slid down to the landing. *I'm going to make it,* he thought. *They can't stop me—*

He turned to continue down the next flight—and drew up short.

There stood four more redcoats, rifles leveled at his chest. They were all scowling; they looked ready to plunge their bayonets into him the moment he tried to escape.

Slowly he raised his hands. One of them stepped forward and ripped the powdered wig from his head. He shook his brown hair free and stared brazenly back. Lackeys like these wouldn't get a word from him, he thought.

Footsteps sounded on the marble staircase behind him. He glanced back to find Lieutenant Trotter descending toward him at a leisurely pace.

From the balcony, the governor raised an eyeglass and peered through it at him for a second. "I trust you'll enjoy our Port Royal prison, Mr. Shaw, or whoever in fact you may be."

Trotter smacked him on the head and everything went black.

4

*T*he last time he saw poor Black Harry Adams alive, thought Quartermaster Blair, had been two days ago, just before Blair had gone ashore for a night of drink and carousing in the numerous taverns that Tortuga's waterfront offered sailors at leisure. "Keep a weather eye for trouble," Black Harry had called to him, and he'd laughed and replied, "Aye, sir, that I will."

He hadn't seen the storm approaching. Though they'd posted a double watch, it hadn't been enough. Dawg Brown's men swam out to the ship at dusk, climbed the hawse in the dark like Indians, and slit the throats of all the men on duty. Peter Sheridan, Jimmy Newkirk, Squint McClaine—he'd lost good friends in that nasty business. It was one thing for a man to die with a cutlass in hand, caught by a cannon's blast or a musket ball in the midst of an honest fight; it was quite another to die quietly in the dark, caught by a knife from behind without a second's chance to make your peace with God.

After butchering the ship's watch, Mad Dawg's real attack began. Fifty of his men stormed through the *Morning Star*, fighting, killing, looting. An alarm went up, but it was too late. More than half the crew was ashore, and by the time they mustered out of the taverns and made it to the boats, Mad Dawg had already finished his work. He'd taken Captain Black Harry Adams by force. When he closed his eyes, Blair could still hear Dawg's mocking laughter carrying over the water.

At least Dawg hadn't scuttled the *Morning Star*. He'd tried to set fire to the powder room, but luckily the fuse had gone out. One small miracle in the midst of disaster.

All that had remained aboard the *Morning Star* of Captain Adams was his dagger, now buried in the mast. Dawg Adams had taken all of Harry's sea chests, from the largest to the smallest. Blair knew he'd been searching for Harry's treasure map, just as he knew he hadn't found it. Black Harry was a clever man, after all.

At least they had the captain's body back now. The ship's sail maker had sewn him up in a shroud that morning; all that remained was to give his body to the sea.

Blair freed Black Harry's dagger from the mast, solemnly wrapped it in a Jolly Roger, then crossed to the body, where it lay by the rail. If only Harry's thrice-damned daughter Morgan were here, they could get on with it.

"She's late even for this," he said sourly to Glasspoole. "We'd best start without her."

Glasspoole shook his head. "Wait, Mr. Blair. I shall bring her." Turning, he strode forward.

Blair frowned: Not a good sign, he thought. Morgan Adams should have been here to say a few words at her father's funeral. She wasn't a tenth the pirate her father had been, and he didn't think much of her assuming command of the *Morning Star*, as Glasspoole had said she intended. Better to seize the ship themselves, he thought. Rightly, Glasspoole or even Scully, the ship's gunner, should have been captain.

John Reed gestured grandly with his pencil. The open journal before him showed a blank page, and he'd been sketching in a chapter heading—an ale bottle. In many ways, he reflected, that one symbol summed up his whole life. John Reed, adventurer, novelist, lady's man—and drunk.

"Think of your freedom, my dear," he said. The words came out a little slurred. "The world's your oyster—you can do anything you want!"

The ship began to shift with a low swell. He leaned back too far, trying to keep his balance, and tumbled out of his hammock onto the floor. Pressing his eyes shut, he let out a low groan. He wasn't sure what hurt more: his head from drink or his back from the fall.

"I must stay here and be captain," Morgan said.

Reed picked himself up a little unsteadily, catching his balance on one of the bowsed-up cannons. He'd strung the hammock between two of them. At first he'd tried to lure Morgan into it for a quick tumble, but she hadn't been in the mood. Her father's death had affected her more than she wanted to admit, he thought, and in many ways he understood. As she drank, he drank with her. Though they ran from different demons, they ran together, at least today.

"Come to London with me," he said suddenly. The old melancholy had come upon him once more. "We'd have such a good time gambling and partying all night. These men won't take orders from you."

"They will." She looked around and caught sight of her monkey. Pulling herself upright, trying to keep a straight face, she told her pet: "You, there—stand to. Hoist my pennant."

Reed had a hard time keeping from laughing as King Charles dropped the empty rum bottle he'd been fingering. It smashed on the deck. Chittering angrily the monkey dashed back a few feet.

"Ham-fisted swab," Morgan said. She gave a wave at the timbered ceiling. "Lay aloft, fetch my spyglass."

Instead the monkey drew a tiny dagger. It chittered at her again, waving the blade like a little cutthroat.

Reed couldn't help himself and burst out laughing.

"Mutiny, will you?" Morgan said sternly. She turned to Reed. "And you, sailor . . . holystone the deck, fore and aft . . ."

"No," Reed said. He folded his arms across his chest and grinned at her. "And you can't make me!"

"I'll lock you in irons," Morgan said. "I'll chain you to a grating and lash your back. I'll—I'll—"

"You'll make me walk the plank?" Then Reed realized what he'd said. He felt his face go red . . . but he was too drunk, and it was too much trouble to be embarrassed. He found himself trying to stifle a laugh. And just as suddenly Morgan was laughing, too. Reed's knees gave out; he fell to the deck again.

A throat cleared. Reed looked up to see that black man—what was his name? Glasspole or Glasspail or something? Glasspoole, that was it—standing in the doorway.

"I'd hoped to find you sober for this, Morgan," Glasspoole said.

"And I'd hoped to be passed out by now, Mr. Glasspoole," she replied just as seriously.

"Important things go on overhead. You should be there."

Morgan nodded. She stood woozily. Then, taking a deep breath, she picked up a bucket of water and poured it over her head. Her dark curls glistened and her shirt clung alluringly to the tight lines of her body.

Morgan shook the water from her head like a dog shaking off the rain. "Lead the way, Mr. Glasspoole," she said.

Quartermaster Blair shifted impatiently from foot to foot. The afternoon sun felt uncomfortably hot on his head; the crew was already muttering unhappily.

Then Morgan and Glasspoole emerged from below and everyone grew quiet. Reed, that drunken poppy friend of Morgan's, stumbled out after them.

Morgan surveyed the assembled crew, then walked forward confidently to join Blair by the rail.

"Here," Blair said, pulling out her father's Bible and handing it to her. It was one of the few things Dawg had left behind. "It were Black Harry's. He'd want you to have it."

"Thank you, Mr. Blair," Morgan said. She accepted the book.

Blair said: "God rest the blessed soul of Harry Adams. May he find peace forever, and a two-reefed topsail breeze." That was the best he could do for his old friend, he thought.

He handed Morgan the Jolly Roger with the dagger inside. She placed it atop the shrouded body, and at her nod two crewmen tipped it into the sea. Blair watched the body sink away; it had been properly weighted and it vanished with almost no splash. A steady stream of bubbles broke the surface for a minute, and then even they were gone.

Blair looked up. Morgan, he thought, looked singularly unmoved by her father's funeral. But then Black Harry would have wanted it that way: This crew would move in on her the moment it sensed weakness.

Scully, the ship's gunner, inched a bit closer to Morgan. His lips bared yellow teeth in a half sneer, half snarl.

"A touching tribute," Scully said.

"We've made our peace," Morgan said, still staring out to see. "I said good-bye when I rescued him."

"Rescue was it?" Scully said. He took another step closer. Blair could see the small scar on the man's cheek turn white—a sign, he'd always found, of Scully's inner rage. "I hope I'm never in distress when you're around."

Scully whirled, raising his hands to quiet the sniggering crew. "Black Harry's gone. I won't speak ill of the dead, but he brought us nothing for months. No rich ships, no cargos, no wealthy passengers to ransom—nothing. We can either sell this rotten barky and divvy up, or you can choose me captain—I have some clever plans that will line our pockets."

Blair studied the crew. They were muttering and shifting uncertainly. Several called Scully's name—but just as many laughed or sneered. Part of him wanted to throw in with Scully—he was an able gunner, a brave fighter, and he feared no one, not even the devil himself—but before he could make up his mind one way or the other, Morgan acted.

She pushed in front of Scully and shouted, "I stand for captain! My father wished it! With his dying breath he told me to take command of this ship and you, the best crew that ever he sailed with!"

Blair heard the surprised murmuring. Nine-Fingers Hambly called, "You're the one what killed him, seeing how you dallied ashore!"

Morgan ignored him. Instead she held up a brown bit of what looked like parchment. As it waved a little in the breeze, Blair saw it had markings on it . . . a map? He frowned.

"As he died, he left this," Morgan said. "It's a map—to Cutthroat Island, the buried treasure of a Spanish gold ship. More gold, jewels, and plunder than you've ever dreamed of."

Someone else shouted. "It's his bloody scalp!"

There were more dubious mutterings from

the crew. Blair squinted, trying to see what the map said.

"What does it say?" Scully demanded.

Morgan looked at the map, moving it closer then farther then closer again, clearly trying to get her eyes to focus. Suddenly she thrust it at her lover, Reed, who had been standing behind her.

He looked it over, turning it upside down, then back again.

"I can't," he said helplessly.

"Why not?" Morgan demanded.

"It's in Latin—an ancient tongue."

Morgan thought it over for a half second. "Then I will get it translated at once—there must be someone who knows Latin at Port Royal. My uncle Mordechai waits with a second piece of the map at Spittalfield. We'll—"

"There's more than one piece . . . ?" someone said.

"Actually, there's three," Morgan answered.

"Where's the third?"

"Dawg Brown has it."

"Well then, it's practically in our pocket," Scully said sarcastically.

"We'll have to fight him for it," Morgan said. "We'll join with Mordechai. Two ships against one—you should like those odds, Scully." She looked out across the crew. "Ask yourselves, what would Black Harry have done? This is our chance to seek some real fortune and pay back Dawg what we owe him at the same time! What could be better than that!"

Scully leaned on one knee and, with a sneer, addressed the crew himself. "We don't even know if there is any treasure. I've heard of Cutthroat Island—aye, and I've heard of Atlantis, too, and the Isle of Mermaids. Remember who you're dealing with, men—she's a born liar."

Those were fighting words, Blair knew. Any man who spoke that way to Black Harry would have found a cutlass through his guts.

"My father wouldn't lie," she said. "That's all that matters."

"Who's captain here should be the best of us. She ain't even close—she's a drunk, a fornicator—"

"I've been known to have a drink," Morgan snapped. "But I'll be sober by noon, and Tom Scully will be a robber of widows for the rest of his life."

With a roar of rage, Scully whirled on her, drawing his cutlass. Morgan pulled hers as well. The crew began shouting, and Blair heard everything from "Gut her, Scully!" to "Have at 'im, missy!"

It was Glasspoole who moved first, though. He stepped between them, raising his hands, bellowing for silence.

"You will not fight!" he said, looking from Morgan to Scully. "Put up your swords!"

Reed said mildly, "I have no vote, being a

passenger, but I might point out that Morgan knows how to use a sextant and Scully does not, so with Morgan, at least you'd have the comfort of knowing where you are."

Glasspoole turned to Blair. "You're quartermaster, Mr. Blair—you decide."

Blair felt utter surprise. He and Glasspoole had always gotten along well, but he had no idea the man placed such faith in him. And what of the crew? Would they stand by any decision he might make?

He moved forward. "Do all agree I do the choosing?"

"Aye," many people muttered; many more nodded their heads. Even Tom Scully, Blair noticed.

Scully was grinning. "A woman captain—we will have curtains on the gunports," he said loud enough for all to hear.

Blair said, "Scully, you're brave and a fighter. No man here would complain if you were captain of this ship. Morgan, I've no great love for you, but if Harry picked you, I'll give you a chance—for a time."

"Two days is all I need: one to Port Royal and one to Spittalfield."

Glasspoole was nodding. "That does not seem unreasonable," he said.

"Two days it is," said Blair. He nodded. That was the right decision. If Morgan could prove herself in that time, then she'd deserve everything she got. If not . . . Tom Scully would be waiting.

A few men cheered openly at the decision. Morgan did have a few supporters in the crew, Blair thought. She'd need them. The rest of the crew, he thought. She'd need them. The rest of the crew looked blackly at Morgan, then over to Scully as if waiting for some signal. Scully, though, made no move as yet.

Morgan took out her own dagger, fingered it for a moment, then turned and threw it in one motion. It struck the mizzenmast next to the spot where Black Harry Adams's dagger had been stuck for the last ten years.

"If any man would challenge me, let him pull that. Port Royal's southwest a point, Mr. Blair. We will make sail. Topsails and courses!"

The crew looked to Blair as if for final confirmation, and, taking a deep breath, he gave it: "You heard her!" he bellowed. "Topmen away, the rest to the braces! We wear ship, lads!"

The sail-monkeys scrambled into the rigging, and Glasspoole moved forward, shouting orders. For now, Blair thought, everyone seemed to have accepted Morgan as captain. Even Scully—though he wore a pained grimace—moved to his tasks. Two days wasn't a long time, Blair thought. But he had a feeling Morgan might yet pull this off. After all, she had Black Harry Adams's blood in her veins.

Morgan had taken up the captain's position, a few paces behind the helm. That jackdaw

Reed stood behind her, watching everyone and everything with a landlubber's awe. The sails dropped, then filled with a loud snap that sounded like a whip's sharp crack. As the ship began to turn, gaining speed, Blair found himself grinning. Morgan just might pull it off.

5

Port Royal, Jamaica

Morgan adjusted her broad straw hat with its long plume of feathers, then brushed the wrinkles from her red silk dress embroidered with white lace. She was a lady today, she told herself for the hundredth time, and come hell or high water, she'd *be* a lady.

"Wait," she said and Reed paused to look back quizzically at her.

"What's wrong?"

"You have to ask?" She rubbed her aching back in an exaggerated motion, then leaned forward to look down at her feet, locked tight in dainty little shoes.

"Just a little bit farther," Reed said.

Morgan took a moment to look up at the

walls of the prison before them. The huge stone and brick expanse looked intimidating. She could scarcely believe their gall in coming here—this is where they'd lock her and her men up if they were caught. Lock her up, she thought, until they hanged her. Her neck suddenly felt tight, and she swallowed.

"It's this damn dress," she said. It hugged her waist and pushed up her bosom, as tight and constricting as a hangman's noose.

They'd taken a small boat and rowed ashore just out of sight of Port Royal, and it had been an easy matter to get into the town unseen.

King Charles chittered on her shoulder, and Morgan stroked his head absently for a second.

"Not a soul," Glasspoole said, a little out of breath.

"In the whole town?" Reed asked incredulously.

"Aye, not a man in a bar or back alley knows a soul who understands Latin."

"I thought Port Royal was a place of education," Morgan said.

"Relative to Tortuga, perhaps it is," Reed muttered.

"Her comes Mr. Bowen," said Morgan.

Bowen, dressed much like Glasspoole, was hurrying down the walk away from the prison's gates.

"I found one," Bowen said the minute he reached them. "There's a prisoner inside what has Latin."

Morgan snorted. "A lot of good that does us!"

"He's about to be sold as a slave," Bowen said.

Morgan felt a glimmer of hope. "Then we'll have to buy him!" she said.

"I'd think," Reed said a little dryly, "that a king's prison would be the last place you'd want to go, but if you're determined, I'll meet you at Spittalfield. I have some letters to post."

"All those correspondents of yours," Morgan said with a laugh. "Very well, Reed. Until tomorrow."

He nodded to her, then trooped down the path toward Port Royal. Morgan turned at once and started for the prison's front gates.

It proved a simple matter to get inside: nobody challenged them, so they simply walked through the gate, across the courtyard, and into a corridor lined with cells.

There was a man in a brown coat stalking from cell to cell with a riding crop, striking prisoners to get their attention. "On your feet—you!" he snapped at an old, grizzled man dressed in rags. Dutifully the man climbed to his feet.

"Show me your teeth!"

The wretch opened his mouth and the man peered inside, made a noise of disgust, and proceeded to the next cell.

"Which is our man?" Morgan asked Bowen.

"The lubber with the riding crop's looking 'im over now," Bowen said.

"Ah," Morgan breathed. She headed in that direction.

"On your feet, you!" the man with the riding crop was saying.

"Ask me politely," the prisoner replied. Morgan strained to see him, but he was sitting well back in shadow; she couldn't see much more than a faint reflected glitter from his eyes.

"What!" the man roared. He brought back his riding crop and swung with all his force.

The prisoner darted from the shadows and caught the riding crop in midair.

"You anticipated too much," the man said. He had a good face, Morgan thought: straight blond hair, high cheekbones, startling blue eyes, and a firm chin. He was dressed in what must have been an expensive suit of clothes, but were now filthy and ruined from time in prison. "It's more like a fencing move—a thrust—" He flicked the crop at the bully, but stopped it an inch from his nose. Then, with a smile, he offered the riding crop back. "It wants practice."

In a low voice, almost a snarl, the man said, "I hope you are fond of pain, slave—I intend to buy you . . ." Turning, he stalked off toward the next cell.

"Now," Morgan said. She strode forward briskly, and she couldn't help but notice how the prisoner sized her up. His expression softened as he relaxed. *He must think I'm some fine lady,* she thought. *If only he knew the truth.*

"Good morning, madam," he said. "As you can see, I'm young, in fine health. I know horsemanship and I write a fine hand."

"I'm told you speak Latin," Morgan said.

"Latin?" He smiled. "Like I was born in the ancient senate—a regular Cicero. Why, do you have children who wish to learn? I'd make a first-class tutor in a tasteful country house—I can do most arithmetic, though I confess to a weakness in long division."

"Stop your chatter and say something Latish," Morgan ordered.

He paused to look her over carefully, as if surprised by her manner. Then he said, "Pulchrissima mulier tu est, et volo lavar pedes tuas."

Morgan turned to Bowen and Glasspoole. Was that Latin? It sounded strange and foreign—not French or Spanish, exactly, but with an echo of both. Her men just shrugged.

She turned back to the prisoner. "What did you say?" she asked.

"You're a very beautiful woman, and I'd like to wash your feet."

Morgan felt herself blush and tried to hide it. She could spark to this one, all right—but she'd vowed no more gentlemen. The naval lieutenant would be her last so long as she commanded her father's ship.

To hide her reaction, she retorted, "You are

neither man nor clean enough." Then she turned, and Glasspoole and Bowen fell into step behind her. She'd found what she was after, she thought. Now it was just a matter of settling on the price.

As the time for the auction approached, Morgan, Glasspoole, and Bowen joined those already within, standing well to the back. Glasspoole kept shifting his eyes suspiciously from redcoat to redcoat; quite a few lingered in doorways or along the walls, carefully watching all that went on.

The auction started promptly at two o'clock. The auctioneer, a portly man in uniform, climbed the steps of a low wooden platform and addressed the crowd: "Today we have thirty-four lots, all prisoners, some for petty crimes and some for debt. We will begin with lot number one, a French tailor. I start the bidding at one pound . . ."

Morgan shifted impatiently through twenty-one men, who went for prices ranging from half a pound to six pounds, two shillings. Finally the man she wanted moved to the front of the stage.

"Next, lot twenty-two," the auctioneer called. "An Englishman and a doctor. Being of value, I start the bidding at five pounds."

"I bid five pounds!" a man's voice called.

Morgan scanned the crowd and spotted the man who'd carried the riding crop. He smiled gleefully at the prisoner, who looked almost pained.

"Ten pounds!" Morgan called.

The man's face brightened as he spotted Morgan. She ignored him and turned instead to the man whose bid she'd just topped.

"Fifteen," he said. A startled murmur ran through the crowd.

Glasspoole moved away from Morgan, into the crowd, toward the man.

"Twenty," Morgan said. She saw Glasspoole bend and whisper something in the man's ear.

The man shook his head and Morgan saw him mouth the words, "Two words in return, nigger—*go away*. That one is mine." More loudly the man said, "Twenty-five pounds!"

"Frog bastard," Morgan muttered. "Thirty pounds!" she called.

Another ripple of excitement ran through the crowd. Glasspoole whispered into the man's ear again, but he waved him away like an annoying gnat.

To Morgan, he called: "Madam, I'll have this man at any price. If you are buying him simply to pleasure you, I offer to do the same at no cost to you at all." To the auctioneer, he said, "Thirty-five pounds."

Morgan headed for the man, slowly easing a dagger from behind her fan. Bowen grabbed her arm to hold her back.

"Captain, I beg you," he whispered fiercely. "Consider where you are—"

Morgan jerked free. What did she care of the danger? Nobody talked to Morgan Adams that way and got away with it!

She reached the man, who smiled. Sweat made his face look oily, and he had a repellent smell. Nonetheless he bowed.

"I hope the lady is prepared to be a good loser," he began.

Morgan lowered her fan and, in a sudden move, jabbed its point into the man's ample rump. He shrieked in surprise and pain.

"What gave you the impression I was a lady?" she hissed.

"My God!" the man cried. "Are you trying to kill me, madam?"

"Yes, that's why I aimed for your brain. Now leave here and go far away, before I cut you to ribbons and feed your carcass to the fish!"

"I tried warning you, sir," Glasspoole said softly.

The man began to back away, his face ashen. Turning, he darted into the crowd. Morgan didn't think she'd see him again anytime soon.

"Forty pounds," she called, "to end the bidding."

"Any other offers?" the auctioneer asked.

Morgan looked around, as did the auctioneer, but nobody spoke up. She nodded; she should have made an example of that fool sooner. It would have saved her considerable money.

"Sold to the lady with the monkey," the auctioneer said.

Glasspoole stayed close to Morgan's elbow for the rest of the auction, but fortunately she did nothing to call attention to herself. Still, he couldn't help but wonder if the damage was done. The prison walls boasted nearly a hundred "wanted" posters for pirates and criminals, and he'd spotted her face among them earlier. She had a hundred guineas on her head. If anyone recognized her . . . that was a lot of money, and the temptation would be great.

When the auction ended and nothing untoward had happened, he began to relax. Perhaps they'd gotten away with it. He accepted forty pounds in gold from Morgan, then went to pay for their prize.

The auctioneer calmly wrote out a receipt, passed it to Glasspoole—and suddenly a redcoat shoved Morgan's purchase over to him.

"My name's Shaw," the man said. He held out one hand, his chains rattling.

"Pleased to make your acquaintance, Mr. Shaw," said Glasspoole. He picked up the chains. "Come on. Our mistress is in a hurry."

Shaw chatted breezily as he walked, but Glasspoole knew he was simply relieved: the Frenchman who'd been bidding on him would not have made a pleasant master, and now Shaw must think he'd found his way into the good life. He'd find out soon enough, though—and Glasspoole allowed himself a rare inward grin.

He rejoined Morgan and Bowen near the gates. And that's when Glasspoole's sixth sense told him trouble was brewing. Troops were being mustered to their left, and they seemed to be tossing more than a few surreptitious glances in their direction.

"Enemy to leeward, Captain," he whispered as they headed toward the gates.

"Forward as well, Captain," Bowen said.

Ahead, guards were forming a cordon at the main gates. Shaw seemed completely oblivious to what was going on. He just kept chattering to Morgan as if they were off to a country picnic.

"Of course," Shaw was saying, "I'm grateful, madam, but I must say you've picked a bargain. I'm connected to all the great families of Europe. I've got a natural pitch for music and a perfect taste in wine . . ." Shaking his head, Glasspoole tried not to listen.

Morgan was nodding slowly. "I see it." She glanced around, and Glasspoole followed her gaze when it lingered on a small door to the outside set in the wall. Then her eyes flicked to two cavalry horses tethered nearby.

Glasspoole understood at once. He nodded.

"I'll go here," Morgan said. "You draw them away. Take King Charles—we'll meet at Dingley Crossroads."

Bowen whistled, and the little monkey leapt to his shoulder. Glasspoole handed Shaw's chains to Morgan, then motioned to Bowen. Together the two men vaulted into the saddles of the two horses. Slashing the reins, they wheeled and charged the redcoats at the main gate, scattering them.

He glanced over his shoulder, expecting to see Morgan slipping quietly out the side door—but instead she was doubling back. Then he saw the problem: more redcoats were swarming in through the door she'd chosen for her escape.

"She's in trouble!" he called to Bowen. "Come on!"

They wheeled and rode back, scattering the redcoats who'd begun reforming their lines and entering the prison courtyard. Quite a few people were lingering with their new purchases or just chatting with friends and neighbors. The whole auction had a festive feel, he thought.

Screaming a battle cry, he rose into the thickest part of the crowd. Men and women shrieked and fell over themselves to get out of his way. Bowen followed.

Redcoats were closing in on Morgan and Shaw. Nearby, workmen had been digging a ditch. Morgan, dragging Shaw by his cuffs, pulled him into the ditch, where she grabbed a shovel and swung it like a club. It downed two redcoats with one blow.

"Have at 'em!" he shouted to her.

Still holding the shovel, Morgan dragged Shaw through the auction crowd. The bidders shrieked and ran for safety even though she wasn't threatening them. Glasspoole laughed. Little sheep, all of them.

An alarm bell began to clang. Glasspoole looked up but couldn't spot it—and knew he probably wouldn't have been able to stop it even if he knew where it was. Faces were already appearing in the windows overhead.

Morgan seemed to be more than holding her own, and more redcoats were pouring into the courtyard. Glasspoole realized they'd have to run now or they'd never make it.

"Come on, Mr. Bowen!" he shouted, wheeling his horse.

They charged for the gate, scattering people like geese.

The fight became a blur to Morgan. She heard blood thundering in her ears and felt giddy, almost drunk.

A construction elevator caught her eye, and she dragged Shaw toward it by the cuffs. She backhanded two more redcoats, and then a horseman charged at her, swinging a saber. Morgan pulled him from the saddle, kicked him in the head, grabbed the weapon away, and pulled Shaw aboard the elevator.

"Hang on!" she said. "Mind your head!"

She slashed the counterweight with the

shovel's blade just as more redcoats reached them. The elevator shot up like a cannonball, crashing into the pulley at the top and letting them off on top of the wall.

Turning quickly, Morgan surveyed the situation below. Glasspoole and Bowen were galloping up a road. They exited through the town's gates. She nodded; they'd be safe enough. That just left her to get Shaw away.

She dragged him along the wall, looking for something—anything—to help her out of this mess.

"Ma'am," Shaw said, "I'm in favor of exercise, but you owe me an explanation."

Morgan ignored him. At a place where the wall divided, she hesitated, then chose her direction: away from the courtyard.

"That way," she said.

She shoved him toward a scaffolding built against the fifty-foot wall. They started climbing down.

Just as they were reaching the bottom, Morgan felt the structure begin to shake. But as the redcoats jumped onto the scaffolding, the planks broke, and they fell in an avalanche of wood and rubble. Morgan pulled Shaw out of the way just in time.

They were in a different section of the complex now—a fancier one, she thought. This had to be where the officers lived.

A fancy carriage was waiting nearby. "Run!"

she ordered Shaw, and shoving him before her, she dashed toward it.

That infernal dress twisted around her legs like some monstrous snake. She ripped the bottom half away, then cast it aside. Her long underwear allowed her more freedom to move, and so what if it was scandalous—she was a pirate, and pirates by definition were scandalous.

She reached the carriage, hauled a liveried black man out of the driver's seat, shoved Shaw inside, and grabbed the reins. Shaw gaped at her.

Hooves thundered behind her. Cavalry had arrived, alerted by the alarm bell, no doubt.

Morgan slapped the reins and the horses started forward with a startled jerk.

Governor Ainslee emerged from the building just in time to see his carriage depart. And the face in the carriage window—Shaw, with a shit-eating grin on his face.

The mounted redcoats galloped up to him.

"He's got my carriage!" Ainslee said. "Mine—that's my carriage—!" Words failed him; he sputtered angrily for a second. "Bring that man back!" he finally managed to say.

The cavalrymen dutifully wheeled their mounts and spurred them after the carriage.

Ainslee couldn't bear the suspense. He stopped one passing redcoat, pulled him off his horse, and heaved himself into the saddle. Kicking the animal, he joined the chase.

In a few moments he caught up with Lieutenant Trotter.

"Don't worry, sir," Trotter said. "He won't get far."

Morgan drove the carriage through the gate as the horsemen closed in on her. She cracked the reins, charging down a narrow street. Men and women dodged out of her way, and chickens scattered with a flutter of wings and startled squawks.

The mounted redcoats crisscrossed behind the carriage, trying to pass it on either side. Some fired their weapons, and several times Morgan heard bullets whistle past her head— too close for comfort. She couldn't let them catch up with her, she knew, of the fight would be over in a few seconds: There were just too many of them.

As a man tried to tried to ride up to her on the left, she veered the carriage in that direction. It scraped against the wall, sending chunks of mortar flying. A second later she let the carriage careen to the other side, hitting the opposite wall. Sparks flew. The carriage jolted and vibrated beneath her.

She glanced back at Shaw to make sure he hadn't fallen out. He was trying to wrench the chains from his wrists.

"Ma'am," he called, noticing her attention, "I'm sensible how occupied you are, but if you have a moment—?" He held up his handcuffs.

In reply, Morgan leveled her pistol at him.

"That seems extreme," Shaw said.

"Get down!" she said.

He ducked—and she fired. She saw a redcoat fall from his horse. That was one down—how many more to go? Too many, she thought.

She tossed the pistol to Shaw, along with her powder flask and bullet pouch. He stared at them blankly for a second.

"Reload!" she ordered.

"It's hard to imagine what part of your life would require me to speak Latin—" he began.

Morgan bellowed, "Reload, damn your eyes, or I'll choke you where you sit!"

Shaw gave her a puzzled look but fumbled the pistol into the right position and pulled the powder flask's cork with his teeth. He began to pour powder into the pistol.

Morgan saw the horsemen pulling up on the other side. Grabbing the reins with one hand, she flicked a horsewhip toward the handle of a passing door. The door flew open and the redcoat's horse stopped short. Unfortunately for the redcoat, he went flying over the door.

Shaw was looking back, an amazed expression on his face. He began to reload the pistol more quickly.

They were almost free of the town, Morgan

saw. A large gate loomed ahead of them. Once they were out, it would be clear skies all the way back to the *Morning Star*.

"Get up there!" she called to the horses, slapping the reins across their backs. They were already beginning to tire, she saw; foam had begun to fleck their glossy coats.

Suddenly three mounted redcoats appeared to block the gate, pistols ready. They raised their weapons and took aim; they didn't move an inch as she barreled toward them.

They're going to let me run them down, she thought with despair.

At the last moment she veered to the side, heading down another narrow side street. The carriage's wheels skittered on the cobblestones for a second, but then they were racing ahead as fast as ever.

"Done!" Shaw announced, holding out the reloaded pistol.

Morgan took it.

"Is it a convenient time to point out that you've stolen Governor Ainslee's carriage?" Shaw asked. "He's right behind us."

Morgan looked back. A richly dressed man was riding in pursuit, closing the gap.

"You're a dead man, Mr. Shaw!" Ainslee shouted.

The street opened up into a marketplace. Unfortunately there was no time to slow down or room to maneuver.

They smashed through one stand after another, ripping through canopies. A wagon broke and sent watermelons tumbling in all directions. They burst through a pen of lambs, and then through a stack of chicken coops. Livestock bolted in all directions.

A canopy fell across Morgan's head, and she tried to rip it away. One of its hooks caught the shoulder of her dress, and when she tore the canopy away, the remains of her once-fine dress went with it. Just as well, she thought; she hadn't enjoyed wearing it, anyway.

"You know," Shaw said, "I'm sorry to put you through all this."

"You . . . ?" Morgan said, caught for the moment by surprise.

"Why, yes, ma'am. I suppose they didn't want me gone after all."

"You self-centered coxcomb imbecile," Morgan said archly. "You have no idea who I am, do you?"

"Lady Something-or-other . . ."

Morgan ripped off her hat. "Morgan Adams, captain of the *Morning Star*."

"The pirate ship?"

"With a crew of seventy-five who follow my orders," Morgan said with pride, "and if you wish to see the sun rise tomorrow, you'll do exactly the same."

"In general, I support the idea of sunrise, of course. I've very rarely actually seen one."

A wider street appeared to the left. Morgan turned the horses into it, leaning her weight to the side to keep the carriage from tipping over. Just as she'd hoped, it led to another way out of Port Royal—a huge arched entryway, its gates standing open for the day, appeared before her.

As they thundered through onto the bridge over the moat surrounding the city, a redcoat jumped from the fort wall onto the carriage. Morgan handed the reins to Shaw and turned to fight the man.

Using the pistol like a club, she clobbered the redcoat in the face, knocking him backward off the carriage. He had a second for a startled scream, and then he was gone.

"Wakes you up, don't it?" she said.

"You're more . . . *active* . . . than any other woman I've known," Shaw said.

Then her road met Governor Ainslee's, and suddenly Ainslee and his four men were galloping behind her. They pulled even.

Morgan frantically reloaded the pistol. Hurry, she told herself as she tamped down the ball and powder with the ramrod.

She raised the pistol and aimed at the closest redcoat, who was getting ready to leap onto the carriage next to Shaw. When she pulled the trigger, the powder inside fizzled—another misfire. Damn her luck!

"They're on the back of the carriage!" Shaw called.

"Take the reins," Morgan said, throwing them at him.

Drawing her dagger, she turned, ready to fight.

"Wait!" Shaw said. He swerved to avoid a religious procession carrying what looked like a mummified artifact of some kind. He shot through a small arch just out of their way.

Ainslee tore through the neighboring arch, where Morgan had seen the procession. The governor couldn't stop in time and collided with the artifact, which exploded into white dust, showering everyone and everything.

"A thousand pardons!" Shaw shouted over his shoulder to the priest.

"That way!" Morgan said, standing and pointing toward a low market roof. The carriage would just fit beneath it.

"But—"

"Do it!" she snapped.

Shaw shut up and drove. With a snarl, Morgan advanced on the four redcoats standing on top of the carriage. Their eyes grew white with fear, and to a man their gazes fixed on the dagger in her hand. Sometimes a reputation for bloodthirstiness came in handy, she thought.

At the last possible second, Morgan turned and jumped with the fluid grace of a panther.

She landed atop the market roof, and momentum kept her running.

She glanced back and saw the four redcoats thrown to the ground. Beneath the roof she heard a horrible clamor as Shaw drove through fish stalls, scattering patrons and fishmongers like a dog among geese.

She ran out of roof and, tucking her head beneath her arm, dove through a window into a ladies shop. She couldn't stop herself and plowed into shelves, shattering bottles of powder and perfume. A dozen high-class women in the midst of dressing paused for a second, staring openmouthed. Morgan knew how she must look—in her undergarments, hair a wild mess, covered in blood from hundreds of tiny glass cuts, with a dagger in her hand.

As one, the women began to scream.

Morgan kept going through the shop, crashing through the far window. She tucked her head down into a roll, and she came up on her feet running. Beneath her she heard more crashing and knew Shaw had followed instructions.

The horses were beneath the edge of the roof, and she kept running toward them, timing her jump so she landed in the seat next to Shaw. He stared at her in amazement.

"Try to stay in your seat!" he said.

"We're not out of here yet."

As if on cue, she heard the familiar booming sound of a distant cannon. She turned and looked out into the harbor. There was a British man-o'-war facing them, smoke trailing from one of its cannons. It fired a second time, and then she heard the telltale whistle of the first cannon ball approaching.

"Keep your head down," she said, "As we're about to become cannon fodder!"

The cannonball struck the building behind them with a terrible explosion, shattering its facade. Sharp bits of stone and plaster rained down, stinging Morgan's arms and the back of her neck. A moment later the second shot hit a tower above an archway, disintegrating it. Dust and smoke filled the air, and flames leapt high into the sky. Men and women and animals ran in every direction, shouting and bleating in panic.

The horses bolted, all but uncontrollable. Morgan gave them their heads—they wanted out now as badly as she did.

She risked a quick glance back. A row of rum barrels caught fire, and as the ropes holding them in place burned through, they went rolling out into the middle of the street. One broke, its contents exploding in a huge fireball, and that set off the others one by one. The street filled with flames and burning rum, and the fire spread quickly into all the nearby market stalls and hay carts. Then a distillery exploded, and the carriage careened out of the way just in time.

"We've certainly left out mark on this town," Shaw said.

"It used to be rather pretty," Morgan agreed. "There goes the neighborhood."

"We should go back," she joked. "There's a part of the town we haven't destroyed yet." And then she laughed long and hard.

6

Governor Ainslee shielded his face from the heat of the fire and pulled his horse up short. Damn Shaw! Through the flames Ainslee could see his carriage disappear around a side street.

His mount was rolling its eyes in fear, so he backed up a few feet. The peasants were already lining up with buckets, trying to put out the blaze—but there would be hell to pay for all the damage. Whose idea had it been to fire on the carriage with a ship's cannons?

Trotter pulled up beside him.

"Who was that Goddamned woman?" Ainslee demanded.

Trotter said, "Morgan Adams, sir. You've a hundred pounds on her head."

"Black Harry's girl—so that's her. She's made me the proper fool, ain't she? Two hundred pounds now, and a captaincy for you if you catch her, Trotter."

Ainslee saw excitement light up Trotter's face. "Indeed, sir." He pulled his horse around and began shouting orders to his men. They galloped off down a side street.

Ainslee had little hope they'd catch them, thought. Black Harry Adams had always had the devil's own luck, and it looked to him like his daughter had it, too.

"I wonder what she wants with Shaw ..." Ainslee mused. There had to be quite a story buried here.

With daylight fading into dusk, Morgan finally came within sight of Dingley Crossroads. She'd been letting the horses walk to catch their breath, but now she urged them back to a gallop.

They thundered up the road to the crossroads proper, and as she drew the horses to a stop, Bowen and Glasspoole emerged from the trees. They'd changed back to their pirate clothes and looked like their old selves again.

Morgan climbed down, then turned and helped Shaw. He seemed a little unsteady on his feet ... and more than a little nervous around his newfound friends.

"Any difficulties?" Glasspoole asked, eyeing her.

Morgan knew how she must look, but she grinned anyway and said, "Nothing out of the ordinary. And you?"

"The same," he said.

"You drive," she said. "I've a mind to sit inside like a proper lady."

He nodded and climbed into the driver's seat, and Bowen joined him there. Shaw, with a slight bow, manacles clanking, clumsily opened the carriage door for her. Ignoring him, she pulled herself up and in.

The seats were of a deep red crushed velvet, and even in the growing twilight she could see the flowery gold and ivory designs painted on the walls and ceiling. The faint, delicate scents of expensive perfumes and snuff lingered like a pleasant memory, and for a second Morgan allowed herself the luxury of relaxing and taking it all in.

Shaw climbed in after her. They hadn't been properly introduced, Morgan thought, studying him through half-slitted eyes. Truly he was a handsome man, or would be when properly cleaned up, with that strong jaw and those piercing eyes. For the second time she regretted giving up men like him.

"What's your name, anyway, slave?" she asked, to get the conversation started.

"William Shaw—Dr. Shaw, in fact, ma'am. And if it's all the same, I prefer the term 'indentured servant'."

"Slave," Morgan began, and she heard Shaw

sigh, "I'm about to show you something. Reveal it to any other man and you'll wish you were back at Port Royal, with your head on the block and the ax in the air."

She reached into her underpants, watching him all the while, his eyes bulged with surprise. She could imagine what he was expecting to see—and it wasn't the scalp of Black Harry Adams. She held the scalp out to him.

"I breathe again," Shaw said with a strangled note in his voice. He took the scalp. "What is this—pigskin?"

"My father's scalp," Morgan said.

A look of distaste crossed his features. He held the scalp away from him with two fingers. "Please!"

"Tell me what's written there!"

"Let's discuss terms first," he said. "I do so and you cut me loose."

Morgan pulled out her dagger and laid it against his throat. She could feel him trembling very faintly against the blade, and his face lost its color.

"Very well—we agree," he said. Morgan removed her knife, and Shaw took a deep cleansing breath. Lifting the map, he tilted it toward the window, studying it in the last dying rays of light. "It seems to be a treasure map," he said.

"I know that," Morgan said. "Tell me what's written there."

"The treasure may be found offshore the island of Haiti in five-fathom water—" he began.

Morgan leaned forward and touched her dagger's tip to his nose, pricking him just enough to hurt—and just enough to get her meaning across. She'd never cut off a man's nose, but she'd seen her father do it, and it wasn't pretty.

Shaw smiled. "I'll take another look," he said with a wink. "Can't blame me for trying." He studied the map again. "Herein lies the longitude of Fingers Adams's gold . . ."

Morgan waited for more, but Shaw didn't add anything. "And?" she finally prompted.

"That's all," Shaw said.

"No position—no parallel?"

"That's all the Latin says."

Rage filled her. He was trying to cheat her again. If he wasn't afraid of a maimed face, she knew what every man feared. She moved her knife away from his nose and brought it down to his groin.

"Lady, I swear it—that's all that's there." She gave him a little poke with the knife, and he added, "Ouch—that's tender!"

"It will get more tender soon," Morgan promised. She glanced down at his crotch, and the reflection caught her eye.

"They're backward," she said softly.

"I assure you, ma'am, they're normal in every respect," Shaw said.

"No, you idiot, the words—they're written backward!"

She turned the shiny knife blade so he could see, too. And there, reflected in the polished steel, hidden in the decorative waves around the island on the map, were more words in Latin.

"Bell me, you're right!" Shaw said.

7

The bookseller's shop smelled of fresh ink and paper, and John Reed basked in the scent. He might be an adventurer, a gambler, and a ladies' man, but first and foremost he was an author. This place stirred his blood like nothing else.

He'd arranged to post his letters on a packet ship bound for Liverpool, and then he'd come here to visit his friend, James Hale, who owned the store. Hale, a short, rounded man with a bulbous nose and ruddy complexion, had thinning gray hair and thick-lensed glasses from too much reading. They made an odd pair, Reed mused, but a good one: he liked to write and Hale liked to read what he wrote. Truly a compatible arrangement.

Reed pulled a sheaf of neatly lettered papers from his jacket and set them on the counter. "My latest chapter," he announced.

Hale picked it up with a look of joy. "I've been waiting for this one, John!" he said. He began to skim the first page. "I'll get this manuscript copied and off to your publisher tomorrow," he promised, "just as soon as I've finished reading it."

"Did you get me that bird?"

Hale set down the papers. "Oh, yes, of course—I nearly forgot. Let me fetch him." He ducked through a curtain into a back room and returned a moment later holding a wicker cage. Inside, perched on a wooden bar, sat a gray pigeon. The bird cocked its head to one side and seemed to regard Reed with some suspicion.

"This is Goliath," Hale said, "and he'll bring as many pages as he can carry safely back to me, no matter where you set him free."

"A whole chapter?" Reed said doubtfully. A pigeon that size looked scarcely able to carry a single sheet of paper, let alone a whole chapter of a book.

"If you write small and on both sides of the paper, yes," Hale said. "You attach it to Goliath's leg with a bit of string."

"I'll try it," Reed promised. He still had his doubts, though. "I wish I could talk more," he said, "but I have my ship to catch."

"More of those special friends of yours?" Hale asked with a knowing wink.

"How else would I get to chronicle their adventures if I didn't sail with them?"

Suddenly the door opened with a jangle of bells.

"Well, I thank you again," Reed said, picking up the cage. "I'll visit again as soon as I can."

"I look forward to it!" Hale said.

Reed turned to go and found his way blocked by a man in uniform—a lieutenant, he saw. The man smiled at him.

"Excuse me," he said, "aren't you John Reed, the author?"

"I am," Reed said. "And you are . . . ?"

"Lieutenant Trotter, sir."

"Pleased to meet you." Reed started for the door. Army officers who so casually knew his name made him uneasy; suddenly he wanted to be far from this shop and far from this man.

Trotter blocked his way.

"What's this about, then?" Reed demanded.

"I've been asked to find you for Governor Ainslee. He's a great admirer of your books."

"The governor, you say? An honor!" He felt his chest begin to tighten with alarm. Much as he would have liked a man as powerful and influential as Governor Ainslee as a patron, such patronages had to be carefully cultivated over the years. An army officer didn't just walk up to you out of the blue and say the governor had become interested in you.

"He's waiting for you now," the lieutenant went on. "If you'd step this way—just for a moment, of course." His hand dropped to the pistol at his belt, but if it was a threat, he didn't voice it.

Nonetheless Reed nodded. He accompanied Trotter to the corner, where a splendid red and gold carriage pulled by four gray horses waited. The driver, a black man in blue and gold livery, kept his gaze straight ahead. Half a dozen redcoats stood by with muskets ready.

Seated in the carriage was a man of middling years in powdered white wig and burgundy surcoat. He leaned forward to regard him with casual disinterest.

"Governor Ainslee," Trotter said, "this is John Reed, the author, currently a chronicler of piracy in these waters."

"Climb in, sir," Ainslee said. "Always a pleasure to meet a literary man." He smiled as he stroked the head of the King Charles Spaniel beside him.

That smile chilled Reed. His faint hopes that this was indeed a potential patron shattered: There was some unpleasantness ahead, and from the way the lieutenant had mentioned "piracy," he had a suspicion it had to do with Morgan Adams.

"If Your Honor doesn't mind," Reed said, taking a step back, "I'd just as soon walk."

"Oh, I insist," Ainslee said. "I can do that, you know."

Lieutenant Trotter motioned to the redcoats, who closed in around Reed. Reed glanced at them, then at the governor, and then he forced a smile. When in Rome, as the old saying went.

"In that case, I'd be honored to join you," he said. He climbed up into the carriage and settled back. Trotter climbed in, too, and sat next to him, hand still on his pistol.

Ainslee thumped the roof with his hand, and Reed heard the driver crack his whip. The carriage jolted forward.

They rode in silence for a good five or ten minutes, and Reed found himself beginning to sweat. The governor just sat and stared at him with that predatory smile locked on his face as if he were about to pass sentence on some unsavory criminal. And suddenly Reed felt like that criminal himself. *But I'm not,* he told himself. *I may have made friends with pirates, but I've never committed a crime myself.*

At last the carriage slowed, and for the first time Ainslee glanced out the window. They had drawn up to a line of gallows, where several dozen bodies hung by the neck, twisting ever so slightly in the breeze.

"Piracy's the scourge of these plantations, as you know, Mr. Reed," he said after Reed had had a good look. The carriage was still moving, but at a slow walk now. "The Crown demands, for the safety of our citizens and their trade, that it be squashed. I therefore offer large rewards leading to the capture of all pirates . . . including Morgan Adams."

The carriage continued to pass hanged man after hanged man. Some were freshly killed; others had been dangling long enough for birds to peck out their eyes. They passed a man painting a newly hanged man with tar to keep his flesh on his bones, and Reed swallowed at the thought of such a grisly chore.

"You seem to think I know Morgan Adams, sir," Reed said. He was a well-known writer, he told himself. The governor wouldn't touch him . . . would he?

"I know you move throughout the pirate world," Ainslee said, "collecting your little tales. If by some chance you came across her, you might tell her on my behalf that I offer her two alternatives. One, an ignominious death on the gallows, like these poor fellows, for mark me, I'll track her down in time."

"And the alternative?"

"She can cut me in for a share of her grandfather's treasure."

Reed tried not to show his surprise. "Why, sir, I'm sure I don't know what you mean," he said.

"I believe you do, Mr. Reed. As you see, I have my own sources. Surprised? Let me tell you something about being a governor. It's not all it's cracked up to be. The Crown wants money out of these wretched colonies—they don't want to put a farthing into them. They give me a great whacking charter with ribbons all over it, and as for salary, why, I'm left to pick up my own profit wherever I can. Do you understand me better, sir?"

He fixed Reed with his stare. Reed felt his uneasiness settle a little; he could understand personal profit as a motive, sure enough. After a second's hesitation, he nodded.

"Good," Ainslee said. "This offer will not be repeated. She can either include me in the Adams treasure or end up a crow's dinner."

The carriage was passing a pirate's body in a metal cage hanging from a pole. Several carrion birds were pecking at the eyes.

"Driver, stop!" Ainslee called. He turned to Reed. "Good day, Mr. Reed—and I do like your writings."

A little unsteadily, Reed opened the door and climbed out.

8

Spittalfield Harbor, Buccaneer Sanctuary

It was a ragged town square in a lawless outpost—night could not hide the crumbling walls and run-down buildings, people drinking and carousing in the streets, constant noise and commotion. And not a redcoat within fifty miles, Shaw thought glumly. Much as Governor Ainslee had tried to kill him, somehow he felt no safety here. He would have welcomed his warm, dry jail cell right now.

Spittalfield Harbor was just Morgan's sort of place, Shaw thought. She climbed out of the carriage, dragging Shaw with her, while Glasspoole and Bowen climbed down from the driver's seat. They stretched stiff muscles but made no complaint. Somehow Shaw thought

Morgan would have little tolerance for that sort of thing. She was shivering a bit; the breeze carried a chill and she still wore only her underwear.

They whispered among themselves for a second, ignoring him, then Glasspoole proceeded up the alley, followed closely by Morgan and Bowen. The monkey named King Charles chittered a bit on Bowen's shoulder, but the pirate ignored the tiny beast and concentrated on pulling Shaw along by his manacles like a recalcitrant donkey. If he planned to try to escape, Shaw thought, this would be his best chance. But he had the distinct feeling that Bowen would not let his guard down for even a moment.

Perhaps he had best hedge his bets by trying to make friends with the cutthroats, he thought. He stepped a bit quicker and caught up with Bowen.

"How'd you come to this line of work, Mr. Bowen?" he asked, interested in spite of himself.

"I was made an orphan," Bowen said, "what with my parents sunk off the Carolinas, and I'd have turned criminal had not Black Harry Adams—Morgan's father—made me a place."

"Well, of course, you *are* a criminal, Mr. Bowen," Shaw said.

"We don't see it that way, since the whole world is crooked, and we're making the best of it we can."

Half to himself, Shaw mused, "So she has a compassionate side . . ."

He stepped up to Morgan and said, "I wondered if you could see your way clear to take these off, ma'am. I'd be eternally in your debt."

"As I bought you and own you," Morgan said, "I'll keep you on a leash. Besides, you'd run."

"No, ma'am, not for the world," Shaw said quickly. "You'd catch me. You'd keelhaul me, whatever that is. Besides, I might choose to stay with you on my own. I find you fascinating."

Morgan just snorted derisively. "Keelhauling is where we drag you under the hull and the barnacles grind you to mush, so mind the fascination. I still can't figure this—read it again."

There was a torch still burning in a holder on a nearby building. Shaw took the scalp and turned it to the light, squinting as he puzzled out the backward letters again.

"On the wicked he will rain fiery coals and burning sulfur," he began.

"Sounds like the Bible," Glasspoole said.

Shaw looked up. "Exactly, Mr. Glasspoole. Psalms eleven: 'When the earth and all its people quake.' Number seventy-five: 'My bones suffer mortal agony.' Psalm forty-two—"

"First Latin, now Scripture," Morgan said with a scowl. "We will have to hijack a priest next."

She stomped forward, and everyone hurried to keep up.

Nathan Bishop watched from the shadows as Morgan Adams and a very odd entourage—two of her men, Glasspoole and Bowen, with a monkey on Bowen's shoulder, plus a stranger in chains—passed close by his hiding place. His eyes narrowed; this was what he'd been waiting for. Dawg Brown had sent him ashore to gather information such as this, and he knew he'd better hurry if it was to do any good to Dawg.

Turning, he scurried through a series of back alleys to a nearby cove, where a small boat waited for him just above the tide line. He dragged it down to the water, climbed in, unshipped the oars, and began to row with long, powerful strokes to where the *Reaper* sat at anchor.

The watch challenged him at once, but he called, "It's Bishop, with news of Morgan Adams!"

"Come aboard," a gruff voice called. Bishop recognized it as belonging to Snelgrave.

As he climbed the rope ladder, a hook reached out and caught his shirt, hauling him the rest of the way up to deck. Snelgrave set him down and smiled a very oily, very unpleasant smile.

"You have news of Morgan?" he demanded.

"She's in Spittalfield," he said, "with three of her men."

"What?" Snelgrave demanded. "Now?"

"Aye, now. I seen her not twenty minutes ago, makin' her way down an alley all secret-like."

Snelgrave smiled again. "This Dawg'll want to know."

Snelgrave went to the quarterdeck and rapped loudly with his hook on the ladder leading up. Muffled sounds of laughter from above broke off, and then Dawg, quite naked, leaned over the ledge to look down. The two whores whose pleasures he had been enjoying peered down a second later.

Snelgrave said, "Bishop's back from Spittalfield. He spied Morgan Adams, which means *Morning Star* can't be far off."

"So she has the map," Dawg said. "You should have told me at once."

"I didn't want to disturb Your Honor's pleasure."

Dawg picked up his cutlass. He gestured at the whores with it, and they squealed in mock alarm. "This isn't pleasure." He held the cutlass up. "*This* is pleasure. Remember that, Mr. Snelgrave."

"Aye, sir," Snelgrave said, grinning. "That I will."

The tavern's windows glowed with a warm inviting light, and laughter and boisterous drinking songs rang from its open doors and windows. A few drunks staggered out; a few more staggered in. Twice pistol shots rang out, and both times laughter followed.

Outside, Morgan paced impatiently. Damn him, what was taken Bowen so long? Had he paused to drink with old friends instead of coming back to report? Scowling, she fingered the hilt of her knife. What could be holding him up?

At last Bowen strolled out like he hadn't a care in the world. He looked up, then down the street, then crossed to the mouth of the alley where Morgan waited with the others.

"Well, Mr. Bowen?" she demanded eagerly.

"Mordechai's in there, scared as a goose," he said. "He must have heard about your father—he's up on a balcony with guards all around him, back to the wall, and he's got his pistols out."

"He's expecting Dawg," Morgan said.

Glasspoole said, "If any of Dawg's men are around, they'll spot you."

"And Mordechai's guards won't let you get close," Bowen added.

"There has to be a way . . ." She studied the building and saw nothing to suggest a plan, then glanced up the street. A few drunks staggered about, and harlots plied their trade in the street and from second-floor windows. A few were laughing and chatting as they waited for customers. A couple of others exchanged sharp words, which led to shoving, which led to an all-out catfight, the women slapping each other and pulling each other's hair.

Whores ... they came and went in complete anonymity. And the way she was dressed, Morgan mused, she was halfway there.

One was headed their way now, hiking up her dress as she stepped over a puddle. Morgan looked her over. About the right size, she thought.

"Hisst!" Morgan said.

The whore paused, looking up the alley. "Who's there?"

"A customer," Glasspoole said. "I'm having a little trouble standing—maybe you could help?"

The whore took a step closer—and then Morgan reached from the shadows, grabbed her arm, and pulled her into the darkness.

"How much?" Morgan asked.

The whore looked at her in shock. Shaking her head, Morgan stripped the woman of her dress and shoes, then had Glasspoole leave her a shilling for her trouble ... it was more than she'd make in a night plying her trade, and the dress wasn't worth nearly that much, anyway.

Morgan noticed Shaw trying to shield his eyes as she pulled it on.

"Am I that ugly?" she asked, half teasing.

"No, ma'am, it's just— I don't feel right—"

She laughed as she pulled on the dress. She

didn't have a whore's makeup painted on her face, but who looked at faces this late at night? The dress—with its provocative low cut emphasizing her ample cleavage—would more than do.

She led the way to the tavern, and the others scurried to keep up. Unfortunately the harlot's shoes didn't quite fit, and she had to keep adjusting them to keep her toes in place. She'd never get used to proper ladies' clothing, Morgan thought. Give her good sturdy boots or bare feet any day.

"Won't these look odd in there?" Shaw said, showing her his manacles.

"Odd?" She gestured toward their whole group—a whore, a well-dressed black man, a young man barely more than a child . . .

Shaw sighed.

When Morgan pushed through the crowd into the tavern's main room, nobody noticed—most eyes were fixed on a large upturned barrel near the center of the room, where a man was seemingly at war with some creature within. A second later a hissing moray eel erupted from the barrel, lashing its tail around a man's arm. Money changed hands; the man screamed and tried to put the eel back. Laughter boomed when it bit him.

Morgan's gaze swept across the room quickly. Every corner of the dive was packed with cutthroats of every description. Some were smoking pipes; others played dice or urinated in the corners. Women carried pitchers of beer and ale to the tables, laughing and joking and letting patrons grab their breasts and bottoms as they pleased. Everything and everyone was for sale in here. She didn't see any of Dawg's men, though, and that was boon enough.

At last, forcing her way through the crowd, she reached the bar. Morgan leaned her elbows on the huge oak slab and called to the tapster, "Pour me a rum!"

"Who are you here for?" he asked, pouring. As Morgan had predicted, he didn't even glance at her face.

"The owner sent for me," Morgan said brazenly.

"That will be Mordechai," the barkeep said, indicating the balcony. "He ain't let no one near him in days. I suppose even an old turtle has his needs . . ." He set the glass on the counter.

"Shoot it for me," Morgan said.

Impressed, the man took a pistol from under the counter, shook out its ball, stuck the muzzle in the glass, and pulled the trigger. The glass filled with smoke.

"You're our kind of woman," he said.

"Is that any good?" Shaw asked, pressing forward to examine the drink more closely.

Morgan slid it toward him with a grin. "Smooth as satin," she said. "Like mother's milk. Go on, give it a try."

Shaw shrugged and picked the glass up. He

stared at it for a second, watching the residue of black powder swirl inside, then threw it back in a quick motion.

A second later his eyes bulged and he choked. He wasn't able to breathe for nearly a minute, and his face turned beet red.

Morgan laughed. "I lied," she said. "You stay put." She glanced at Glasspoole and Bowen. "Watch him closely."

The tapster poured her another drink, shot it, and slid it to her. Picking it up, she headed up the stairs toward the balcony.

She felt her heart starting to pound in her chest as she reached the top and turned to the right. There were half-curtained alcoves all along this part of the balcony, and bodies writhed in carnal pleasure within them. She barely glanced at them as she passed; she knew Mordechai would never let down his guard in such a way. They had to be minor officers from other pirate ships anchored nearby.

At last she reached a more somber alcove where several men stood guard, hands on the pistols in their belts. She started to duck through the curtain, but one of the guards caught her arm.

"Where do you think you're going?" he demanded.

"The tapster sent me," she lied. "Said the old turtle has his needs. If he don't want me, there are plenty more who do."

The other guard, giving her a quick once-over, turned and stuck his head through the curtain. "Captain, you in the mood for a whore?" he asked.

Mordechai Adams, looking old and tired and somewhat the worse for wear, stuck his head out to see. He had her father's hair and eyes, Morgan thought, but his grizzled face seemed worn. His worried, frightened expression brightened a bit, and he gave Morgan a leery smile.

"I hadn't thought of it—but now that you're here, 'twould be rude to send you away. Shake her down," he said to the guard who'd called him. His head disappeared behind the curtain.

Morgan raised her arms and stuck out her rump, and as the guard frisked her, his hands lingered on her breasts and buttocks, exactly as she'd planned.

"You're sweet," Morgan whispered in his ear, "but all that usually costs money."

The man took out a gold doubloon and showed it to her; she shook her head.

"I'll take care of you later," she said.

She swept past him, through the curtain, and into the room where Mordechai waited with half a dozen of his most trusted men. It was exactly as Bowen had described it. Mordechai himself stood with his back to the wall, his guns out, clearly afraid. The rest of Mordechai's men weren't much better. They were a grizzled lot, and to a man they wore the expressions of the doomed.

"Sit here, girlie," Mordechai said, indicating the edge of the table. "Give me your little hand, as I'm in need of some womanish comfort."

"In front of all these men?" Morgan asked, feigning shyness.

"Bless me, I think this one is shy!" Mordechai said.

Morgan gave him her most appealing look, and he leered back. Then he nodded once and waved his men away. "Out with you. I'll call when I want you."

When they left, he pulled his chair close to Morgan, took her hand, and pulled it toward his crotch. "And now show me your little skill," he said softly.

Morgan pulled her hand away. "That would be unnatural, Uncle. People would talk."

"Uncle?" Mordechai said.

Morgan pulled a pistol from under her dress and pointed it at his head. "Call your men and it's the last sound out of you," she said.

Mordechai eyed her closely. "Wait—I know you!" he said. "You're something familiar to me . . . you're Harry's girl, Morgan. It is you, ain't it, you blasted unlucky wench. You always was trouble—now why are you here?"

"I've brought my father's map," she said.

"You have it? What of the ship?"

"She's mine—I've taken command."

Mordechai's eyes widened as Morgan pulled

out her father's scalp. "It's his blessed head!" he said.

"His piece of the map as well. Now show me yours."

"Oh, that. Unhappily, it's gone. I lost it somewhere—I misremember."

"You're lying," Morgan said. She would have beat the truth out of a lesser man, but Mordechai was her uncle . . . and one of the few good things she remembered from her childhood.

"Well, what do you expect, damn you?" he said. "Dawg's already done two of us . . ."

"You're scared," she said accusingly. "I expected more from you, Uncle."

"Of course I am!" he snapped. "Why have I spent my life halfway around the world, in Madagascar and the Bight of Benin? I'll tell you—to avoid that murdering bastard. Only a fortune could tempt me back, and if you're here, you've no doubt brought him as well."

"But there's two of us—Dawg's only got one piece of the map. Here, look at what I'm doing—is this not fine?"

She put her piece of the map on the table and smoothed it out so he could see all the details.

"Aye," Mordechai said slowly, "that's handsome of you." He leaned forward and looked it over for a second. "And aye, it fits mine . . ."

"Then put down yours and we'll shake

hands. I'm not afraid of Dawg, and I'm half your age and nowhere near the sailor."

She held out her hand. He eyed it.

"You shame me," he said. "I don't like that." He looked at his own hand. "When you're young, you wish a million things. When you're old, all you wish is to get older. I'd heard of Cutthroat Island before—I thought it was a sea story. Piles of skulls, reefs made of sailors' bones. I never knew it was my own dad's gift to me."

Suddenly he tried to take her hand away. "You make a fine whore—you sure you're not one, playing games with me?"

Morgan shoved him away, hard. "You shame your name, Uncle."

"You're right—there's no water in Adams blood," he said. "All right, I'll do it—I'll shake hands and join with you."

He took her hand and shook it, and Morgan was pleased to find his grip strong. Perhaps there was a little more to him yet than she had thought.

"Like Harry," he said, "I kept my piece of the map where nobody could ever find it. This way."

Turning, he led the way out of the alcove.

As Morgan slid through the curtain, a chain suddenly whipped around her neck and dragged her back off the rail. She smashed through a table on the main floor, and for a second the whole world exploded with bright lights and colors. She tried to shake her head clear and stand, but someone knocked her back down. Her gun went flying—she was disarmed.

"It's Dawg!" she heard Mordechai gasp somewhere close by.

The chain around Morgan's neck tightened painfully, and she tore at it with her fingers to no avail. Someone hauled her up to her feet, and suddenly she found herself staring into Snelgrave's foul face.

"Unfinished business from the other night, girlie," he said with a laugh.

Morgan tried to hit him, but she could barely draw a breath and felt her knees going weak on her.

Suddenly Snelgrave whirled her around. A dark figure was entering the tavern through a seaside tunnel, outlined against the sea. Slowly he walked down the stairs into the tavern.

It was Dawg, Morgan realized. When he stepped into the bar, the room went utterly silent.

Snelgrave released the chain. Slowly Morgan got to her feet. As Dawg approached, she whipped a knife from her bodice and threw it at him.

Dawg batted it out of the air with his cutlass. "Anything more, Morgan?" he said with a sneer. "Empty your armory, dear niece."

Morgan stepped back. She couldn't help it;

Dawg suddenly terrified her. She glanced around for help, but saw none—Dawg's men had already disarmed Glasspoole. Shaw was backing up. Bowen was trying to disappear into the shadows, and even loyal King Charles had covered his eyes with his paws.

Dawg glanced up at the balcony, and Morgan couldn't help but follow his gaze. Mordechai was being lowered from the balcony by Snelgrave's chain, his hands around his neck to keep from choking.

"I knew you'd bring him," Mordechai hissed. "Blast you, Morgan!"

"Well met, brother Mordechai," Dawg said. "All my surviving family and all of Fingers's map, together in one room." He grinned at Mordechai, who cringed.

Then he turned toward Morgan, advancing. "There's a certain value in being the bastard," he said. "Few things rarely surprise you— you're rarely disappointed. For example, I'm going to ask you for your piece of the map, Morgan."

"You can ask until hell freezes over and then keep asking!" she snapped back.

"Wonderful," he said. "I knew you'd say something like that—and that we'd fall to oaths and various bloody threats. I find all that tedious—I look to cut through it. I value efficiency." He turned, surveying the room slowly, and his gaze lingered on the eel barrel.

"Ah, just the thing," he said. He plunged his

hand into the eel barrel and yanked out a hissing eel, holding its neck as it slapped its tail.

"Hold her," he said to Snelgrave and Bishop, and the two men seized Morgan's arms and pinned her. Slowly Dawg advanced, holding the eel before him as its tail lashed this way and that.

Dawg held the eel's snapping jaws near Morgan's face. She tried not to cringe, tried not to breathe. She felt her whole body beginning to tremble. She had never been so terrified in her life.

"This says it all, Morgan," Dawg said. "Viciousness. Pain. Mutilation. My coat of arms . . ."

"He even looks like you," Morgan managed to say with a little of her old fire.

She forced her gaze away from the eel's fangs. Her eyes locked with Shaw's, and he grinned and gave her a wink. Just like him to gloat, she thought.

And then Shaw picked up a candle from the top of the bar, dropped it onto the floor, and suddenly flames exploded everywhere.

9

*A*n explosion suddenly rocked the tavern. Everyone was jolted, and for a second Morgan found herself free.

Dawg wheeled, cursing, and a second explosion sent him staggering off balance. Morgan grabbed the moray eel by the tail and swung it like a club, hitting Snelgrave in the face. He screamed and reeled back as the eel sank its fangs into his cheek.

Fighting had broken out all over—brawling, knife-fighting, swordplay. Several pistols fired, and men went down with screams. A table behind Morgan suddenly broke to splinters as two men from the balcony fell onto it, still grappling.

Shaw blew up the rum barrels, Morgan realized suddenly with growing admiration. Her slave had a lot more gumption than she'd given him credit for. He could have stood there, not saying a word or doing anything, till Dawg left . . . and then he would have been completely free. Instead, he'd tried to save her.

She couldn't let the opportunity go to waste. She strode through the smoke and fighting, looking for Mordechai.

She finally spotted him struggling with Dawg, who suddenly whipped out a knife and put it to his neck.

"I'll have your map, brother," Dawg said. "You know me—I never give up and I never give in!"

Suddenly Snelgrave appeared before Morgan, his face a bloody mess. He screamed at her and charged, and she stooped quickly to get the broken leg of a stool. It was the only thing at hand.

His momentum forced her back toward the shattered remains of the bar. Frantically she parried, parried, and parried again. He was using the chain on his stump to whip at her, and for a second she wondered if he'd best her. But then she noticed him beginning to tire, and she knew she had the edge.

Suddenly she launched a dazzling attack of her own, pounding savagely at his head and face and arms, forcing him back into the center of the fray. Snelgrave, retreating, stumbled over a corpse and fell backward, but before she could finish him off a mass of struggling bodies rolled between them. When they passed, he was gone.

She spotted Bowen cowering in a barrel. "Back to the ship, Bowen!" she called to him. "Bring the men!"

Bowen climbed out of the barrel, ducking as a pirate almost slashed his throat with a cutlass, then dodged off through the pandemonium. He'll be back in fifteen minutes, Morgan thought. She just had to hold her own that long.

Where was Glasspoole? There, off to the side—dueling with one of Dawg's men in a vicious, no-quarter fight. He seemed to be holding his own.

Suddenly Morgan heard a roar behind her and saw Snelgrave, back on his feet, rushing toward her. Frantically she looked around for a cutlass, but there was none at hand.

"Morgan!" she heard Shaw call, and she glanced in his direction in time to see him lobbing a cutlass toward her.

She caught it, turned, and blocked Snelgrave's attack and suddenly two more of Dawg's men were on her. She had no choice but to give ground, parrying frantically. There were just too many of them.

She found herself backing toward Shaw. "Better arm yourself, Mr. Shaw!" she said.

"Easier said than done, ma'am," he said. "Do you think you might unlock these now, given the circumstances?"

Morgan parried and riposted, cutting one man in the shoulder; with a curse, he fell back. "I don't have the key," she called.

"Where is it?" Shaw demanded.

"They never gave me one!" She ran the second of Dawg's men through, and that left only Snelgrave for the moment. She advanced on him, her sword a blur, probing his defenses.

She backed him to the stairs to the balcony, and as he whipped his stump-arm back, fighting to keep his balance, the end wrapped around a post. He was tethered and he didn't know it. This was her chance, Morgan thought.

Another pirate jumped into the fight, but she ran him through, then stepped past Snelgrave's defenses and punched him in the face with the cutlass's guard. He fell across the bar, dragging shelves full of bottles down on top of him.

Raking in deep breaths, Morgan turned to survey the scene. Glasspoole had just sent one of Dawg's men crashing into the eel barrel, and now hissing, snapping eels wriggled across the floor, looking for places to hide. Across the bar, Mordechai, in Dawg's grasp, suddenly lunged forward and impaled himself on Dawg's dagger.

"No—" Morgan gasped.

Dawg regarded his half-brother's body for a second, then let him drop. Turning, he neatly ran one of Mordechai's men through with his sword. His gaze swept the room, and when his eyes met Morgan's, he grinned.

Morgan felt a cold wind chill her spine. She flinched.

"I saw that, Morgan," he said, advancing on her. "I remember from when you was small. Always flinched when you saw your uncle Douglas, didn't you? Give me Harry's map now or regret it—"

Morgan retreated, throwing barrels, chairs, even people into Dawg's path to keep him at bay. He kept advancing, like an unstoppable force. One of Dawg's men was looting a body, and she grabbed his arm, whirled him around, and threw him at Dawg—and the man found himself impaled on Dawg's cutlass.

"You'll not get away!" Dawg screamed at her as he tried to wrench his blade free. It seemed to be stuck between two ribs, Morgan thought.

There was nowhere for her to go but up. Leaping over some barrels, using a man as a stepping stone, she vaulted over a divider into a private booth.

Behind her, she could still hear Dawg Adams cursing.

Shaw had thrown himself to the ground the minute the fighting got out of hand. He'd found a cutlass, but Morgan had needed it in her battle so he'd thrown it to her.

Then he'd watched the pirate captain—Dog? Was that what they were calling him?—grab the other, older captain and place a knife to his throat.

Shaw crawled closer, straining to hear.

"The map, Mordechai, or I shall peel you like an apple!"

"It's lost," Mordechai said. "Don't kill me, Dawg— For the love of God—"

As he watched, Glasspoole threw one of Dawg's men into the eel barrel, shattering it. At that moment Mordechai lunged forward, impaling himself. Dawg let him drop and started after Morgan.

Shaw saw his chance. Rising, he darted toward the wounded pirate, skirting fights and trying to stay out of harm's way.

Mordechai, crawling as best he could, made it to the shattered eel barrel and began digging through the broken bits of wood. Shaw reached him, but stood well back—there were still eels in there, biting and hissing, and several of them had punctured Mordechai's arms.

Mordechai hardly seemed to notice. With the last of his strength, he pulled out the bottom piece of the barrel, pulled it to his chest—and died, a half smile on his face.

Shaw reached out, trying not to touch any of the eels, and gently pried the piece of barrel free. When he turned it over, he smiled in recognition: It was the second piece of the treasure map.

There was a picture of part of an island burned into the wood, and one written line: MAY CRUEL DEATH LEAVE VICTIMS IMMORTAL.

Shaw stuck it in his pocket and headed for the stairs near the bar. Suddenly he drew up short—the stairs were blocked by a cadre of advancing pirates, and they looked none too happy to see him. Swords drawn, they headed straight for him.

A rope hung nearby. Grabbing it, he used it to swing wide of them and up onto the balcony. Rather than letting the rope go, though, he tied it there—he didn't want them using his trick to follow him.

Motion caught his eye, and he whirled in time to see Morgan grab a chandelier filled with burning candles and swing across the room, over the fight, and toward the balcony. A pistol shot rang out, but the ball went wide, missing Morgan.

Gritting her teeth, she landed catlike before him.

"You have something of mine, I believe, Mr. Shaw." She raised her cutlass to bar his way.

"Upon my word," Shaw said, "I don't know what you mean."

Two of Dawg's men fell on them from either

side. Shaw trusted Morgan to dispatch her attacker, but he had serious doubts about his—he was unarmed and manacled still. But the half-drunken pirate didn't prove as much of a threat as he'd thought. The man closed with him too quickly, and he stepped inside the man's guard and, even in his manacles, managed to wrench the man's sword away.

That made it a better match. He drew on his fencing skills and assumed the proper stance; the pirate drew a long knife and faced off against him.

He attempted a quick attack, trying to throw the man off balance, but he moved more quickly when his life depended on it. Stamping his foot, Shaw executed a textbook lunge, only to have it parried away. He met the riposte, then countered with a feint and a thrust.

"Very pretty, Mr. Shaw," he heard Morgan say behind him.

"Thank you, ma'am," he said. "I had the good fortune to study with a grant-master in Vienna . . ."

"But at some point, you might stop diddling and kill the bastard."

"Kill him?" Shaw said with a laugh. "Bless me, we never got to that!"

From behind, Morgan grabbed his sword-arm and shoved the blade into the man's stomach, a simple, direct blow.

"I see," Shaw said, wrenching the blade free.

It made a grating noise of steel on bone that set his nerves on edge.

Morgan ran to the balcony railing, and Shaw followed. Below, Glasspoole stood on a table fighting off three or four attackers. He moved with a panther's speed.

"Morgan—make for the tunnel!" he shouted.

10

Morgan whirled, looking for a clear way to the sea tunnel. There didn't seem to be one. She'd have to cut her way out, she thought.

She spotted Dawg across the room, his dark eyes fixed on her as he fought his way through several of Mordechai's men. He moved almost effortlessly through the carnage, killing one man, then another, then another, using his pistol as a club and his cutlass like a scythe.

He'd be there soon if she didn't move fast. Turning, she headed for the stairs at the far end of the balcony. One of Dawg's men—she recognized him as the one who'd helped Snelgrave hold her down—rushed at her from the side.

Snarling, she butted him with her head, grabbed his crotch, and flipped him backward over the railing. He hit the floor with a satisfying thud, but Morgan barely noticed—she was already leading Shaw down the stairs.

"Come on!" she shouted to Glasspoole.

Mr. Glasspoole leapt off his table, running toward her, and Morgan took the opportunity to slash the chandelier rope. The chandelier plummeted, demolishing the table on which Glasspoole had been standing and flattening the knot of men around it. The burning candles set fire to spilled rum on the floor, and a line of flames raced toward the broken casks of rum stacked to the side. A second later they exploded, sending a huge fireball throughout the center of the room.

Morgan shielded her face until the brightness died down, then peered out, trying to see what had happened. Everything was burning. More than half the pirates were on the floor, either dead or unconscious. Behind a wall of flames she thought she could make out Dawg, shielding his face but still trying to get through.

"Hurry, Captain," Glasspoole said, touching her arm.

Morgan turned and led the way down to the sea tunnel. The tavern used it for storage; demijohns of rum and ale were stacked on either side nearly to the ceiling. Torches guttered smokily in holders along the walls.

As they advanced, the air lost its musty earthiness and grew fresh with the smells of the sea. They'd made it, she thought with relief.

Then she drew up short. What was that sound? She held up her hand and everyone behind her grew silent. Coming toward them from the shore exit she could hear loud, boisterous talking. Someone was in the tunnel.

Shaw said, "Your men, Morgan?"

"I think not," Glasspoole said, easing to the side. He picked up a demijohn of rum and lifted it over his head.

"What—" Shaw began.

"Get back!" Morgan cried, turning and heading toward the tavern at a run.

Shaw followed.

When Morgan glanced back over her shoulder, she saw Glasspoole heave the demijohn of rum at the archway where the torch was flickering. The barrel burst, splashing rum everywhere, and the torch ignited it with a loud explosion.

The men coming in from the shore began to shout in panic. Glasspoole, ignoring them, ran to join Morgan in the main room of the tavern.

Flames were everywhere now. Morgan looked frantically for a safe way out and finally spotted a high window. If they could just make it up there . . .

"That way!" she shouted, pointing.

Beginning to climb up the wall, she found

hand and footholds. Shaw and Glasspoole followed. Once Morgan looked back and found Dawg glaring at her from behind the wall of flames. She swallowed and kept going.

Outside the window was a balcony, and from there a rope bridge led to the next building. Morgan helped everyone out, then turned and started down the bridge. At that moment she felt a sudden bite of pain and caught her breath in surprise— She'd been hit. She didn't know how badly, though, and she wasn't about to slow down enough to find out.

Just then a stack of rum barrels suddenly blew up in the tunnel. A huge fireball billowed behind them, blasting out the window. Aflame, the end of the rope bridge sagged toward the ground—Morgan was barely able to leap onto a narrow walkway.

Climbing onto it, the three ducked as the windows exploded out behind them from the heat.

As they sprinted forward, two of Dawg's men suddenly blocked the way. There was room for two to stand here, and Morgan and Glasspoole faced off against them together.

These were younger, less experienced pirates, Morgan thought, feinting then running her man through. No wonder Dawg hadn't brought them inside. She shoved the dying man off the balcony, and Glasspoole's followed right behind.

They reached the corner of the walkway and

rounded it, only to spot half a dozen more of Dawg's men rushing toward them.

Morgan looked back. More of Dawg's men were closing in behind them. They were trapped.

Another explosion rocked the building. Morgan wheeled. It was her men from the *Morning Star* finally come in answer to Bowen's summons. They had a small cannon and were firing on the tavern. Dawg's men were cowering and covering their heads to protect their faces from debris.

Her men had bought them some time. Morgan looked at the building across from them, but it was too far to jump. Then she looked down.

Below and a little to the side sat a hay cart—probably fodder for horses in the tavern's stable. But it would more than do.

"Jump!" she said, and, without hesitation, she took a step and leapt. She landed in the hay and rolled, them climbed down behind the cart. Shaw and Glasspoole jumped, too, and she helped them down.

The square was full of Dawg's men fleeing the fire. Several ran to the burbling fountain and took cover behind it, firing at Blair and the rest of the *Morning Star*'s crew. Morgan winced as she saw one of her men fall.

More of Dawg's men came running to hold Blair back, but a well-aimed coconut grenade exploded in the fountain, swamping them with a huge geyser of water. That should soak their black powder, she thought with satisfaction. They wouldn't be shooting their pistols now, which should give her men a decided advantage.

Keeping close to the buildings surrounding the square, Morgan led the way to join the rest of her crew. Dawg's men soon spotted her and rushed them, and then she and Glasspoole were fighting for their lives.

Blood roared in Morgan's ears. She cut, thrust, cut again, forcing her way inexorably forward. This was for her father and her uncle, she vowed, and suddenly she was in the clear again. She glanced back in time to see Glasspoole finish off the last of Dawg's men in the group.

"Ma'am," Shaw breathed, "I've never seen fighting like that!"

She gave Blair a quick wave.

"My compliments!" she heard him shout over the roar of pistols and the clang of swords.

She was about to try a quick run across the square to join him when she spotted Bowen laying down his cutlass before one of Dawg's officers. She sprinted over and ran the man through with her blade, then wrenched it clear.

"This does you no good on the ground, Mr. Bowen," she said, flipping his cutlass back to him.

Bowen looked mortified, but managed a quick nod.

Glasspoole and Shaw raced up to join her, and then they all raced for the sea entrance. Behind them, the rum barrels that had collapsed the porch exploded in another huge fireball, lighting the square as bright as day.

Morgan stopped suddenly, staring up at the sign for a fortune-teller's shop. Everyone else drew up short, too. Lit in reds and oranges from the burning tavern, she could read the word PALMS above the door. The sign, a wooden hand with the fingers pointing up, had heavy lines across the palm and fingers. Each line was numbered.

"Begging your pardon, ma'am," Shaw said, "but this is no time for fortune-telling!"

"What were those numbers?" she demanded.

"Numbers?" Shaw asked.

"The psalms!"

"Eleven, forty-two, and seventy-five," he said.

"No time for that now!" Glasspoole said, seizing her hand and pulling her along.

"I figured it out!" Morgan said. "They're the longitude!"

All of her men were retreating through the square's huge archway. As Blair joined them, he slashed at a rope holding a cargo net full of coffins. The falling coffins smashed, spilling disease-ridden bodies. The wreckage blocked the alley, leaving them a clear escape ahead.

"This may stop them altogether," Glasspoole said, grabbing a hanging lantern and lobbing it into the alley. It shattered, splashing burning oil onto the walls.

Douglas "Dawg" Brown strode through the burning tavern, a vision from hell. His eyes, reflecting the light of the fires around him, smoldered a blood red. Smoke and soot blackened his skin; sparks, caught in his long coat, smoked and smoldered.

Kicking open the door, he walked out into the courtyard. For a second he turned, surveying the carnage around him. Bodies littered the street. Far off, a dog barked frantically, then grew silent. He heard no sounds of fighting—no sounds of people at all. The town might have been deserted.

He noticed a corner of his coat on fire, and he casually brushed it out, like a man brushing away a fly. It mattered little to him.

Revenge, though . . . that mattered a lot. Morgan Adams would pay for this. If she thought he'd been hard on her fifteen years ago, wait till he had her in chains in his cabin now. Death would seem a release.

Morgan felt the tension like a knife between her shoulders. As she raced down the beach toward the longboats waiting above the tide line, dawn broke in the east, coloring the sky with pink and yellow fingers. It had been a long night.

She helped her men push the first longboat out into the waves, ignoring the pain from the wound in her side. She climbed in and sat in the stern, in the captain's position. Glasspoole and Bowen helped pull Shaw aboard, and then they settled at the benches and helped the rest of the crew begin to row them out to where the *Morning Star* waited at anchor.

Forcing a grin, she said, "Brave work, lads—we taught Dawg a lesson he won't soon forget. And I've found Cutthroat's longitude— Psalms seventy-five, forty-two, and eleven. Cutthroat lies seventy-five degrees, forty-two minutes, eleven seconds west."

"Dawg won't be far behind," Blair said.

Morgan saw Shaw's interest, and for a second he slacked off on his oar.

"Put your backs into it!" Morgan called.

"Why don't you row . . . ?" Shaw muttered.

"Why don't you swim?" she countered, and that shut him up.

Ahead, the men standing watch aboard the *Morning Star* saw them and began to wave.

Quieter now, feeling the pain in her side, Morgan sat back and waited until her longboat pulled up beside the ship. The watch let down a rope ladder, and she climbed up and surveyed everything. It all seemed just as she'd left it. She nodded slowly. Exactly as it should have been.

"Set sail, Mr. Blair," she said as soon as everyone was aboard. "Southwest a point west, for the time being."

Blair turned and bellowed, "Cut along, lively now—we've not time to waste!"

Then Morgan turned and found Reed waiting. He looked her over critically.

"You've been in a fight," he said. "Are you all right?"

"It's just a scratch."

"I'll tend to it as soon as we're under way," he promised.

"No need," she said. "I know how the sight of blood affects you." She turned to Shaw. He was staring at her with a bewildered and slightly bedraggled expression. "Now you . . ." she said.

"Ma'am?"

She hooked the arm of a passing crewman—his name was Flemming, she recalled.

"Make sure he don't move an inch, Flemming," she said. He nodded. "And get somebody to cut off his chains."

Shaw grinned. "Thank you, ma'am!"

Morgan looked up. As sails unfurled and sheets tightened, the *Morning Star* heeled and gathered way. Salt air filled her lungs; the tang of brine drove the taste of land from her. This was the life for her, she thought, feeling bouyant inside.

Nodding, sure that for once everything was under control, she headed for her cabin. She made sure she walked with a swagger, the way a pirate captain ought to, the way her crew expected.

Inside, she closed the door, crossed the cabin, and slumped into her father's chair. King Charles chittered to her happily from his perch on the desk.

Unwrapping her wound, Morgan studied it critically for a second, then picked up a rum bottle, pulled the cork, took a swig, then poured a liberal dose on her wound. Half-and-half, they called it: half inside, half on the wound, battlefield medicine at its finest.

The rum burned like a white-hot brand, inside and out. She winced.

"And not a word from you!" she said to the monkey. He had been staring at her.

Rising, she looked over her father's Bible, his charts, his parallel and dividers, his spyglass. As she touched them, a million thoughts ran through her mind. How could she ever hope to measure up to him? How could she ever take his place?

No, not take his place, she told herself. Never that. Live up to his name—yes, that was better.

Bowen knocked twice, then stuck his head in. "Need anything, Captain?" he asked.

"Bring up my gear, Mr. Bowen, if you please."

He nodded and headed off—but he'd done something good for her. He'd called her captain. She took a deep breath. If she was going to be a captain, it was time to act like one.

She spread out her father's chart of the Caribbean. Using dividers and parallels, she plotted the longitude line.

"Seventy-five . . . forty-two . . . eleven . . ." she murmured.

She drew a pencil line down the length of the chart. The line crossed a cluster of islands labeled "Crooked Man's Keys." On the map beside them were the words "Bad water—reefs and coral heads." Just the place, she thought, if you wanted to hide an island like Cutthroat . . .

11

*S*omething wasn't right, Dawg Brown thought. For a second he paused, listening to the wind and the feel of the ship around him. We aren't moving, he realized. A pale dawn light streamed in through the porthole above his head. Why—

Growling under his breath—somebody was going to pay for this—he climbed onto the deck and strode toward the forecastle. A knot of sailors stood helplessly around the capstan and the anchor hawse. He saw several of them pale and take steps back. Well, he thought, gut one of them and the others would toe the line straight enough. His hand dropped to the sword at his belt.

Bishop stepped in front of him. Dawg drew up short.

"Why aren't I moving?" he demanded again.

"The anchor's fouled," Bishop said.

"Cut it loose."

"Aye—" Bishop began.

But one of the sailors from the capstan stepped forward. "We can't leave yet, Captain," he said. "We ain't put enough food aboard—"

Dawg hardly glanced at the man. Idly, as if he were swatting a fly, he drew his pistol and plugged the man square in the chest. The pirate fell backward, gave a gurgle and a twitch, and then lay still.

"Fewer mouths," Dawg said, "less food. Does nobody hear me on this ship? I distinctly said, *Cut it loose!*"

Nobody moved. All of his men were staring at him, mouths gaping. Even Bishop, poor fool.

Dawg snarled, climbed to the forecastle, grabbed an ax, and raised it high. The crewmen around the hawse scattered. But he'd had his taste of blood for the morning; he couldn't afford to waste any more men.

With a grunt, he brought the ax down with a mighty whack. The anchor rope split and went whistling away down its hole and into the water below.

"Let's go!" he roared, ax still in hand. "We have a tide to catch!"

Men were scrambling in the rigging. The *Reaper* began to move . . . but still not fast enough, Dawg Adams thought, shaking his head. They'd wasted half the morning tide already.

His ship was faster than the *Morning Star*. But not when she lay safe at anchor in the bay!

"More sail!" he bellowed. "Make time, there! More sail or I'll hoist your innards over the mizzenmast!"

His men doubled their efforts.

Morgan changed into breeches, boots, and a plain shirt in her cabin, then slipped half a dozen knives into various hiding places in her clothes. Lastly she tucked a pistol into her belt. With two pieces of the map, she thought, she had a fairly good chance of keeping the crew in line, at least for the moment. As long as the crew smelled gold, they'd follow her—exactly as her father had promised.

For once her head didn't ache and her vision remained as keen as a hawk's. The perils of drink . . . but oh how good it tasted at the time.

"Come on," she said to King Charles, and chittering happily the monkey climbed onto her shoulder. Then, taking a deep breath, she pushed open her cabin's hatch and went out on deck.

At once King Charles scampered off into the rigging . . . just in time to miss Scully, who hurried over. He seemed to have been waiting for her, Morgan thought. Well, he wouldn't find her a grieving girl today—she was in command here and meant to stay there.

"The second map, Morgan," Scully said. He seemed to be trying to be polite and charming . . . and failed utterly. "We're all very interested to see it."

"As am I. Watch carefully, Mr. Scully," she said.

Deliberately she turned her back on him. Normally that would have been a very dangerous thing to do, but she knew nothing would happen to her until she produced the map. And in the meantime it showed the crew she had no fear of him.

She searched among the watchers until she spotted Shaw. A crewman was just parting his chains with a sledge and chisel.

Rubbing his wrists, Shaw nodded and grinned at those around him. "Much better, lads," he said. "I thank you most kindly."

Morgan drew up before him. "Take off your clothes," she said.

"Ma'am?" Shaw said, looking puzzled. Probably can't believe he heard that right, Morgan thought.

"Remove," she said, "doff, strip. Clothes away, Mr. Shaw—which part of it don't make sense to you?"

"You mean *here*?" Shaw asked, looking around at the ring of men surrounding them.

"I don't see why not."

Shaw swallowed and looked at the circle of

hard faces. They weren't half as hard as her own, Morgan thought.

Shaw must have decided the same thing. He quickly unlaced the front of his shirt, took it off, and dropped it to the deck.

"Ma'am," he said, "please—"

Morgan said, "If I was to ask you, Mr. Shaw, what you took off my uncle Mordechai's body at Spittalfield, what would you say?"

"You saw?" Shaw asked, pausing.

"I did—you're not half as clever as you think."

Shaw gave her a quick grin. "You impress me, ma'am, I must confess." With a sigh, he reached into a back pocket and pulled out a jingling purse, which he handed over. "Eyes of an eagle, to be sure."

"What is this?" Morgan asked. It had to be some trick. She hadn't seen him take a purse.

"Why, that's your uncle's own purse, which I pinched. You may well ask, what sort of fellow robs a dead man? I'd answer, the kind that's been jailed and must start over from scratch."

So, the pouch was Mordechai's—but it wasn't what she needed. An added bonus, nothing more.

"Enough games," she said, motioning with the pistol. "Trousers!"

"Perhaps if you told me what you were looking for?"

"My uncle Mordechai's map, which you lifted."

Shaw raised his hands. "Never, madam! I did no such thing!" He looked imploringly at the crew around him. "Gentlemen, the lady's mistaken—"

This was getting them nowhere. Morgan calmly cocked her pistol and took careful aim. Just as easy to search a dead man, she thought.

Shaw must have understood her intention. He quickly stripped off his pants, then held them defensively between her and him.

"Is this fair?" he demanded. "I remind you I helped you escape Port Royal, and I started the fire in the tavern—"

"Less talk, more removing," Morgan said.

Shaw handed over his pants. He was left standing in strange-looking baggy shorts. The crew started to hoot and catcall, and Morgan had a hard time keeping a straight face herself.

Quickly she felt through the pants. Nothing in the pockets . . . nothing sewn up in the lining . . . nothing, nothing, nothing! She felt her anger bubbling up inside. Would he really draw this out so ridiculously? It seemed so.

"Your smallclothes," she said.

"Morgan!" Shaw said, aghast.

"All the way down to the strakes and rudder, Mr. Shaw," she said. "There are many places to hide things."

"I beg you," he said, "leave me one shred of dignity!"

"Do it, or Mr. Blair will do it for you . . . and you have my word he is none too gentle or patient, Mr. Shaw."

Shaw swallowed but stripped off his shorts and threw them down in front of her. Quickly he covered his privates with his hands.

Morgan poked his undergarments with the toe of her boot, but they were empty. Then she circled Shaw, looking him over. He had grown red around the face and throat from embarrassment. Nothing there, she thought.

"You see?" Shaw said as she continued to study him. "Nothing. Well, something, but nothing that does not belong there."

Morgan looked at his face. She became acutely aware of everyone staring at her, wondering what this was all about. Damn it, she'd seen Shaw take something! He's hidden the map somewhere aboard ship, she thought. That had to be the answer.

"What's your choice, Mr. Shaw—hung by your thumbs and dangling from the mainyard, or towed aft like a log?"

Shaw opened his mouth, but a shout from the mizzen crosstrees interrupted.

"On deck, there!" the lookout shouted. "Sail, hull down, dead in our wake!"

Morgan rushed to the taffrail, and everyone on deck joined her. She pulled out her spyglass and trained it on the distant sail. Though she strained, she couldn't quite make out the ship. But she had a bad feeling about it.

"Can you make her?" she shouted up to the lookout.

"It's the *Reaper* bark, all right, with the bit in her teeth, wearing every sail she's got."

"He's found us fast enough," Mr. Glasspoole said from beside Morgan. "Do we fight him?"

"He outguns us," Blair pointed out. "It would be suicide."

"We'll fight him when the time is right," Morgan said. "Until then, topgallants and staysails, Mr. Blair."

Blair turned and began shouting orders to the crew, sending some aloft and others to fetch the rarely used topmost sails from storage lockers.

Morgan raised her spyglass and turned to gaze aft again. One thing at a time, she thought. Let Shaw think she'd forgotten him . . . perhaps he'd let down his guard . . .

Aboard the *Reaper*, Dawg stood in the forepeak gazing through his own spyglass. They'd made up for the delay already, he thought. Morgan wasn't half the sailor her father had been . . . he'd run her down soon enough.

"She sets topgallants and staysails," Bishop said from behind him.

"It will not help her," Dawg said. "We're faster. Sail on, sweet Morgan—wherever you go, there I'll be . . ."

*M*organ Adams, ready to take on the world.

Photo by David James © 1995 Carolco.

*W*illiam Shaw develops a taste for adventure.

Morgan receives
bad news about
her father.

Photo by David James © 1995 Carolco.

Photo by David James © 1995 Carolco.

Morgan rows
to his rescue,
but is she in
time?

*O*n Cutthroat
Island.

*M*organ rallies
her crew.

*M*organ and Shaw get to know each other. . .

. . . *A*nd join forces to find the treasure.

*S*haw is captured by Ainslee and his men.

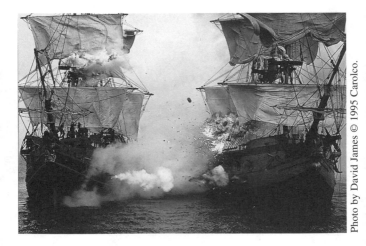

*B*attle on the high seas!

*M*organ swings into action.

*M*organ's dagger holds surprises.

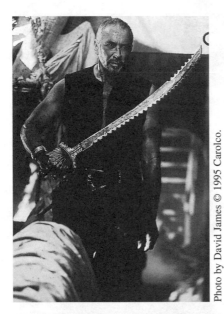

Bloodthirsty Dawg Brown wants the treasure—and revenge.

Photo by David James © 1995 Carolco.

Photo by David James © 1995 Carolco.

But Morgan is taking no prisoners.

12

*T*he answer lay in the charts, Morgan thought.

She brought Glasspoole, Blair, and Reed below to her cabin and spread out the chart. As she leaned forward, she felt a twinge in her side and grimaced; she'd almost forgotten her wound in the excitement. Well, she couldn't let it slow her down—Scully was waiting for his chance, and Dawg wasn't far behind.

"The line I plotted runs here, through Crooked Man's Keys," she said. "Cutthroat can't be far off. Look at the chart—'reefs and coral heads.' Dawg outguns us, yes, he's bigger—but that makes him heavier, don't it, and he draws more water. We'll lure him into the keys and run him aground on the coral heads. We'll kill him there and take his map."

She watched as the others considered her plan. Slowly they began to nod. They saw it, too—it just might work.

Her side gave another twinge, and as she touched her side, she felt something wet—blood. Then her body let her down completely; she found herself growing light-headed and started to fall. She tried to catch herself on the chart table, but her hand left a bloody stripe across the chart as she fell, darkness washing over her like a tide.

The next thing she knew, she was in her bed. Reed was rubbing her hand, a worried look on his face. Glasspoole and Blair stood to the side, murmuring softly to themselves, arms folded.

"Wha—" she began. She realized she'd fainted. And if she was in bed, that meant they had put her here, and discovered her wound. Morgan felt herself blanch. Flemming might serve as ship's doctor, but he had no formal training save what his midwife mother had taught him as a boy. As often as not his cures killed.

As if on cue, Flemming appeared in the doorway. He had a red-hot poker in his hand.

"You're sure that's necessary?" Blair demanded.

"It's festering, that's why," Flemming said.

"Can't you take the ball out?"

"Hard to say. Best I seal up her side with

this hot poker—that's what we always do in such cases."

A new voice interrupted: "No offense, gentlemen, but given the circumstances, don't you think this calls for a professional?" It was Shaw, Morgan saw with a measure of relief.

Blair moved to block his way, but Glasspoole caught his arm.

"Let him through," Glasspoole said, "he's a doctor."

When Shaw stepped forward, Glasspoole led him over to Morgan. Slowly he bent to examine her wound, probing gently with his fingers. It shot lancets of pain through her whole side, but Morgan bit her lip and made no sound.

"I'll need surgeon's tools," Shaw said to Blair. "Hot water, sulfur, and clean packing. Some rum might help the pain."

Blair hesitated, looking at her. Shaw seemed to know what he was talking about; his cure couldn't be any worse than Flemming's. Morgan nodded slowly.

"See to it, Mr. Blair. And why is everyone standing around here? Who's sailing the ship?"

"Come on, everyone out," Blair said. He shooed everyone toward the door.

Only Reed hesitated.

"You as well, John," Morgan said softly.

Reed gave Shaw an unreadable look—but he turned and followed the others out.

* * *

Shaw waited nervously, holding Morgan's hand, until Blair managed to find all the materials he'd asked for. He didn't know what had made him speak up—he was no doctor, after all!—but it had been his instinct, and he'd always gone by instinct in the past.

Morgan, in bed with her side bared toward him, took another long drink of rum. At least she seemed to be getting drunk, he thought . . . but whether that would help or not remained to be seen. If anything happened to her, he had a feeling Reed, Blair, and the others would string him up for revenge. But if he cured her . . . If he cured her, he just might pull through this whole adventure alive, in one piece, and rich as old King Midas himself.

He poured rum over the wound, and Morgan thrashed a bit in sudden pain, her jaws and fists clenching. But she did not cry out. She was tough, he'd give her that. *I'd be screaming in her place*, he thought.

Holding up the pair of clumsy tongs Blair had provided for him, he took a deep breath. *Better get on with it*, he thought. He swallowed.

"Uh, this is going to hurt, ma'am," he said.

"Get on with it!" Morgan said. She took another long swallow from the rum bottle.

Shaw leaned forward and inserted the end of the tongs into the wound. It was an ugly, gaping mess, and its smell made him faintly nauseous, but he wasn't about to give up now. Too much was at stake. Call it job training, he told himself. Anyone could be a doctor, after all; how hard could it be to remove one bullet?

His hand slipped and Morgan howled in agony. Shaw jerked back, startled and afraid.

"Clumsy swab!" Morgan said.

"Sorry, sorry," he murmured. He'd better be more careful, he thought. He inserted the tongs again, feeling for the round hardness of the bullet.

"*I* was supposed to torture *you* . . . Ow! Do you see it?"

"Close—another minute—"

He snuck a glance at Morgan's chart on the table. It seemed to show an island or group of islands . . . though there was a lot of blood there. What was the name? He glanced back at her.

It seemed his interest in her charts hadn't gone unnoticed. But she didn't say anything. Instead she took another long sip of rum, watching his eyes rather than his hands.

"Your father and two uncles each had pieces of the map," Shaw said. Perhaps she was drunk enough that she'd tell him everything if he phrased it right. "The treasure, it's large, I take it?"

"The largest ever taken," Morgan said. "A Spanish gold ship— Ouch!"

"Sorry, sorry," Shaw said. "And a third uncle chases you? An unusual family."

"Would you like to know just how unusual my uncle is, Mr. Shaw?"

He nodded, studying her wound. That glint of silver-gray—was that the ball? He thought so.

Morgan continued, "He has a scar on his neck—runs halfway around at least. A few years back, some of his crew didn't like the way he was treating them, so they decided to mutiny. Well, they were all so afraid of him, they knew their only chance of success would be to kill him. They tried poisoning first, which had no effect. So one night when he was sleeping, fifteen of them went into his cabin. The plan was to whack off his head with a boarding ax. They hit him all right, severed his neck, but not clean through . . . a fatal mistake. Dawg held his head on with one hand and laid into them with the other. Those what survived, he boiled alive and ate their hearts in front of the rest of the crew, with a relish of pickles and pineapple. I'm told that some of them still have nightmares about it."

Shaw gave an involuntary shudder. "I'm sorry I didn't have the chance to know him better," he said sarcastically. Then the tongs gripped something hard, and he pulled, extracting the lead ball. "Success!"

He dropped the ball into a pan with a loud clinking sound. Morgan looked relieved; she sank back on the bed, the lines on her face easing a bit.

That just left the matter of the wound. He took a handful of yellow sulfur and dusted it over the raw flesh. It must have stung, for she took a sudden intake of breath through her teeth and leaned away from him.

"What's wrong?" she asked.

"Some experts recommend sutures; some do not. I am of two minds."

She leaned back to look up at him. "Do whichever will help me back on my feet soonest."

"More toward me, if you don't mind," he said.

"Sorry, Mr. Shaw." She leaned toward him again, and her breeches slipped down a little, showing quite a bit of her thigh. He couldn't help but notice several small tattoos on her hip: one rose, and beside it five teardrops.

"A rose and teardrops . . . ?" he asked.

"That's none of your business."

"Who can you trust, if not your physician?"

She hesitated, then said, "Tears are for the men I've killed. Roses are for lovers."

"You've killed five men?" Shaw asked, surprised in spite of himself. From the way she acted, he hadn't been able to decide if she'd killed hundreds . . . or none at all.

"I stopped counting," Morgan said.

"Only one rose—you stopped counting?"

"No," she whispered, "I started." She gazed at him, and he saw a softening in her expression. "I've treated you cruel, haven't I?" she asked.

He tried to brush it away. "You've had a lot on your mind."

"And you did help me," she said, "at the prison . . ."

"And the tavern," he said. He gave her a smile and started to bandage her wound. No sutures, he decided; he didn't like the idea of sewing a wound closed, anyway.

"Let's say between us, for argument's sake, that you have Mordechai's map," she said.

"But I don't."

"I know," she said, "but pretend you do. I was willing to go halves with my uncle and his. I'd do the same with you and yours."

"You're saying," Shaw said, "that if I showed you mine, you'd share yours with me. We're asking whether we can trust each other."

Her voice grew huskier. "You should trust me more," she said seductively, "having seen me underneath."

"Underneath," Shaw said, "you're without equal . . ."

"And . . . ?"

"But on the surface, you're a slave owner. If I did have the map, it might be the only thing keeping me alive. Hand it over and you'd have no more use for me."

"I cut your chains," she said. "Why, do you think . . . ?"

"To stand me naked in front of a shipful of men?"

"Other possibilities . . ."

"Because you wanted to take a better look?"

She smiled, lifting her head, and Shaw found himself growing aroused. Was this what she wanted? Was it what *he* wanted? Her lips were so inviting. He bent close.

"Maybe," she whispered. "Give me the map . . ."

"Give me a kiss, first . . ."

She closed her eyes and lifted her face toward him. He bent and touched his lips to hers. It was more than he expected—perhaps more than she expected, too. She seemed to soften beneath him, and then she threw her arms around his neck.

He pulled her to him, and she gave a sudden sharp intake of breath. He'd touched her wound, he realized.

"Sorry," he said.

They parted, and he stared into her eyes. He'd always found himself a good judge of people, but for once he could see nothing in her face, nothing in her expression, beyond the surface.

"Now the map," she said softly.

"The thing is, I don't have it." Better to be safe, he thought.

"Ah," Morgan said wistfully.

"That's not to say we can't keep talking about it," he said quickly.

He leaned forward to kiss her again, but she turned away. Before he could decide what to do, a rap sounded on the hatch door. A second later Bowen stuck his head in.

"Talk to yourself," Morgan said. "Yes, Mr. Bowen?"

"Mr. Blair's respects, Captain—*Reaper*'s five miles off and closing."

Morgan pushed Shaw away and stood a little uncertainly. He reached out to steady her, but she pulled away.

"You shouldn't get up yet," he said.

"Mr. Bowen, see that Mr. Shaw gets a change of clothes from the slop chest. He is beginning to stink."

Bowen nodded and indicated the hatch to Shaw. Nothing to do but go along, he thought. She had been using him. He'd almost been fooled, and now he was glad he'd kept it to himself.

As he left the cabin, he glanced down at the charts again. He'd have to get back in here sometime soon. And, as Bowen escorted him aft, he heard Morgan muttering to herself, "He has it. He lies like a Persian rug."

Shaw swallowed, remembering her threats. It seemed his reprieve was only momentary.

13

The *Morning Star* sailed through a tight cluster of small islands. The sky overhead had become the gray of old slate, and the air held an electric undercurrent that promised a tropical squall. The sun, already sinking to the west, left them with perhaps a half hour of dusk ... enough, she hoped, for their escape.

Moving slowly, she climbed to the poopdeck. Blair had men cleaning and priming the cannons, she saw, in readiness for a battle. As they noticed her, the crew muttered to each other, grinning and laughing, then threw themselves into the work with a new spirit. Indeed, everyone seemed pleased to see her up and about, she thought—even Scully. They needed someone to look to in times of trouble, and they had accepted her as that someone.

Things were going to come out right in the end: She felt it in her heart and soul. With the bullet out of her side and a good plan to follow, they had little to worry about beyond finding the treasure. Though she remained weak, the dizziness had left, and she no longer felt sick.

She headed aft to the taffrail. "Where's Dawg now?" she murmured to herself. Drawing her spyglass, she gazed aft. The *Reaper* had drawn much closer. "Exactly where we want him," she whispered. "Keep following me, Uncle."

Aboard the *Reaper*, Dawg Adams stood in the forepeak gazing at the *Morning Star*. Two miles, he thought, and closing fast. Another hour and he would have her.

"She makes for Crooked Man," Bishop said beside him.

He nodded; he could see that well enough. "She hopes to tear out our bottom on the coral." It was a plan worthy of her father, he thought.

Snelgrave, to his left, said, "Looks like we're in for a blow, Captain. Should we attack her now?"

"No," Dawg said. "We'll go around the islands in the dark and then ambush her on the other side at daybreak. She's clever, our Morgan. But I will catch her. Every Dawg has his day."

Morgan turned to find John Reed standing before her, swaying ever so slightly with the movements of the ship. He reeked of rum. It wasn't his normal drink, but aboard ship he made due.

"I'm using this piratical stuff for a book—I admit it," he said, his words slurred. "I'd never let it use me—put me in physical danger, for example."

Morgan looked him over. Same old John Reed, she thought.

"This life isn't for you," he went on. "You're much more like . . . me . . ."

"You?" Morgan chuckled.

"In the sense of living for fun, without a care in the world." He drew himself up straighter. "A pair of adventurers and hedonists, two like souls, two leaves drifting in the river of time . . ."

Was that how he saw her? Was that how she saw herself? Once she would have agreed, she thought, and joined him in his drinking. But now . . . now things had changed. Now she had people depending on her. Now she had a promise to keep—to her father and to herself.

"You should have been a poet," she told him, to change the subject. She felt uncomfortable with him, suddenly.

He was too drunk to notice. "In my early

days, I was a poet," he said. "But I was never a very good poet. There were always too many better than me . . . so I set out to find my own way, to follow my own path and all the rest of them be damned!" He laughed. "And so I have become famous!"

Morgan turned and gazed aft. It was growing hard to see the *Reaper*. Another five minutes and it would be completely dark.

Dawg's men began lighting lanterns for the rigging. She watched as first one, then another, then another yellow glow appeared. It seemed he wanted her to know he was following . . . as if that could intimidate her.

She had to admit it was working. She took a deep breath and tried to still the pounding of her heart.

Shaw crouched by the longboat, out of sight of the crew. This was his chance to take another look at his piece of the map, but still he hesitated. With everyone busy, it was probably safe. But if anyone came along and caught him, it would be plain what he was up to, and he'd lose his piece of the map.

The temptation was too great. Finally he gave in and pulled the hidden map out of the boat. The sky was cloudy and growing darker by the minute. Leaning back, he tilted the map to catch the last of the sun's light and examined it closely for the first time.

Across the top were a series of words in English: "May Cruel Death Leave Victims Immortal." May—that was a month. He counted on his fingers: "March, April, May—" Then he shook his head. That wasn't it. He had no idea what it meant.

Perhaps it was a code . . . but what could the words stand for? "May" could be "mais" in French, but "cruel" . . . ?

Slowly he began to puzzle through the possibilities.

"Why do you think I've stayed aboard all this time?" John Reed demanded.

Morgan, scarcely paying attention, didn't even look at him. "For your stories, I suppose," she said.

"Not only that. *More*. You know . . ." He paused as if tongue-tied, and when Morgan still did not look at him, he grabbed her hand.

"Is it that fellow Shaw?" he demanded. "Just because he has all that hair? You know my feelings, though I haven't exactly said them out loud."

She pushed his hand away, feeling uncomfortable. She didn't want to face this particular problem now.

Then another thought struck her. What about Shaw? She hadn't seen him in a while . . . and she remembered the way he'd looked at her charts.

Bowen stood nearby. She said to him, "My slave, Shaw—has anyone seen him?"

Bowen shook his head. "No, Captain." The others nearby muttered and shook their heads, too.

He had to be up to no good, Morgan thought. Turning, she left the poopdeck to find him.

As she passed Glasspoole, he said, "Can't see the horizon—a storm's coming our way, off the islands."

Shaw let himself into Morgan's cabin and lit a taper from the low-burning oil lamp. He used it to light a candle, which he carried to the chart table. Leaning forward, he studied the chart on top, the one marked with a bloodstain.

To one side, half buried by papers, he saw a corner of another map . . . Morgan's part of the treasure map. He tugged the corner gently, exposing it, then pulled out Mordechai's piece and put the two together.

They joined, but they made no sense to him. What good was a map without plain instructions?

He stood and looked around the cabin for another clue, something—anything—to help him. There were various journals and logs lying on tables around the room; one of them, with John Reed's name on it, caught his eye. The date said "1670"—and under it, written in Roman numerals, the same date: "MDCLXX."

"May Cruel Death Leave Victims Immortal," he breathed softly, knowing he'd found the key.

"My word. $M \ldots C \ldots D \ldots L \ldots V \ldots I$. Fourteen degrees latitude, five minutes, six seconds north."

Using his fingers as dividers, he took a dimension off the side legend and lay it on the longitude line Morgan had already drawn on her chart. He found the intersection readily enough, but there was nothing in the place but open ocean. Had he missed something? He measured again quickly.

The sound of a pistol cocking—loud as a bell in the stillness of the cabin—stopped him short. He looked up and found a pair of eyes regarding him from the shadows.

"No, you were right, it's uncharted," Morgan said, moving forward. "Where did you hide the map?"

Shaw sighed and let his shoulders slump. "In the boat. Under the seaty thing." He'd win her sympathy, pretend to play along, he thought.

"I knew you'd wind up here at some point," Morgan said, "that chart being the cheese and you being the rat. 'Fascinated' with me, Mr. Shaw? 'Without equal' . . . ?"

"You see my problem, ma'am. I'm basically a shallow man." He gave her a tentative smile. If that didn't do it, he didn't know what would.

"And no doctor either, or am I wrong?"

"Not really. I'm surprised you let me fiddle with your side."

"And no gentleman, either," she said.

He shrugged a little. "I wanted to be both, but unfortunately was born poor, and so I'm really only a thief and a liar."

"Since you lie so easily, and since you are so shallow, we shall have to lie you in a shallow grave." She threw back her head and called, "Mr. Blair . . . !"

"Have you no charity, ma'am?" Shaw asked. "You a pirate, me a thief—it's not so far apart . . ."

"I brim with charity, Mr. Shaw," Morgan said. "I am charity's very soul."

Blair entered and stopped when he saw Shaw being held at gunpoint.

"Success, Mr. Blair," Morgan said. "My slave has found Cutthroat Island. Mark it on the chart, slave, since you can."

Shaw picked up a pencil and made a large cross at the intersection. Morgan stepped forward, spun the chart around, and stared down at it.

"And being so charitable," she went on, "I'll maroon you on a rock the size of this table instead of splattering your brains across my bulkhead, the way you deserve. Take him below, Mr. Blair."

Shaw let his shoulders slump, but inside he felt a brief bit of hope. He was still alive, and she didn't intend to kill him. That, at least, was a beginning. Things could only get better if he played his cards right . . . and he played them very, very well.

* * *

John Reed stood staring into the darkness. With the storm coming on, the air had taken on a charged, electric feel. It would be quite a storm, if he was any judge.

What had happened between him and Morgan, he wondered. He'd thought he'd found in her a kindred spirit, perhaps even the woman he wanted to spend the rest of his days with. But now something had happened to come between them, and he wasn't quite sure what it was.

Lightning lit up the sky, and a clap of thunder followed. The wind picked up; the choppy water began to grow heavier.

He decided he'd better get below. As he headed down the steps for the cabin he shared with Morgan she came out. He stopped for her, hoping for a quick word, a sign perhaps of her returning affection, but she brushed by him as though he wasn't even there.

Melancholy filled him. Reed knew then that he'd lost her. She was no longer the same Morgan Adams he'd loved. Shaw had done it.

A sudden rage filled him, and he stomped down and burst into the cabin. He swayed a bit as the ship rocked, and as he steadied himself on the chart table, his gaze fell on the large *X* marked in the middle of the ocean.

He realized at once what it meant. She'd found Cutthroat Island.

Well, leave him she might, but he'd do his best for her. She wasn't the pirate her father had been. If she found the treasure, Dawg or Ainslee would take it from her ... and hang her for her trouble. Best to throw in with Ainslee, he thought, and be spared the gallows' rope.

He pulled out a sheet of paper and painstakingly copied down the coordinates. King Charles chittered at him from his perch overhead, but Reed only smiled. Once he'd saved her, perhaps she would come back to him. . . . It was the only way.

Scully, tying down the last of the cannons against the storm, watched through slitted eyes as Morgan Adams swaggered across the poopdeck. Fighting the roll of the ship, she caught the rail next to Blair and Glasspoole.

"A bad blow, to be sure!" Glasspoole said over the roar of the wind. "We're reefed down. Best point up into it!"

"I've found it, Mr. Glasspoole!" Morgan said. "I've fixed the island! I know where it is!" She turned and faced into the wind. "It lies through the storm!"

Blair said, "You risk the barky if you head for it."

"I risk Dawg if I turn back," Morgan said. "Shorten sail all you want, Mr. Blair. We'll hold this course."

Scully ducked his head and pretended to finish tying down the cannon. So, she'd found Cutthroat . . . interesting news indeed . . .

He hurried aft. As the storm broke with its full fury, lightning flickered and thunder rumbled all around them. A vicious rain slanted down, all but blinding them.

Around him, the crew manhandled the lines as waves began to break over the gunwales. Blair, shouting orders, sent men aloft to shorten the sails. The mast had already begun to creak dangerously.

Scully found several of his supporters and pulled them aside. They huddled together near the main deck as waves continued to break over the side.

"She takes us into the storm," Scully said to them all. "We should be running from it. I heard her say she's found the island—I say we take the ship and her chart and give them to Dawg. I've no taste to fight him—if we make a gift of the island, think of his gratitude. He'll make us partners."

The others agreed.

John Reed fought the roll of the ship as he tied a note to the leg of one of his pigeons. The note gave the coordinates of Cutthroat Island.

Turning, he threw the bird into the air and watched until it vanished into the darkness overhead.

"There," he whispered to himself, "does that make you feel better?"

It didn't.

14

*T*he storm was growing worse, Morgan thought. As she and Blair burst into her cabin, the ship rose on a new swell, tilting violently to the side. Everything went flying.

She reached the map table just as a huge wave crashed through the stern gallery window, swashing it. Water sloshed everywhere, covering them both.

As the water receded, Morgan showed Blair the chart. He stabbed his finger at the *X* Shaw had made.

"I won't run!" she said. "Look how close we are!"

"The rig can't take it!" Blair said.

"It can—we've been through worse with Harry before. Have faith, Mr. Blair, and trust the ship! With your help I can do it!"

She saw the hesitation on his face. Then he nodded. "All right—we'll try it."

She took Harry's scalp map and Mordechai's piece and stuffed them into her shirt.

As they turned to leave, the hatches burst open. Glasspoole came in—but backward. A crowd was after him, and at their head stood Scully with a sword to Glasspoole's neck. The men with Scully seemed equally well armed.

"What is this?" Morgan demanded.

"I won't drown in a storm for your pleasure, Morgan. We're taking the ship."

"There were too many, Morgan," Glasspoole said.

Morgan set her feet. "Tom Scully, there's no great love between us, but don't do this, not this close. Look—here's the island. It can't be more than two or three leagues off. Don't lose hope now!"

Scully snatched the chart from her hand. With a grin, he examined it briefly, then turned to his men. "This is it!" he said, raising it. They cheered.

Morgan knew they were distracted by the chart. She made a quick motion to King Charles, and the monkey hid himself.

"Take them!" Scully cried, and the men grabbed Morgan, Blair, and Glasspoole, bundling them up and out the hatch.

"Away the longboat!" Morgan heard Scully cry, and she had a bad feeling inside about what was to come.

Perhaps it would have been better if they'd just killed him, Shaw thought. Blair had taken him belowdecks and lashed him to a cannon. Water was dripping in through the gunports; it was ankle deep already and rising fast. The constant crashing waves, the near darkness, the water—he felt more terrified than he ever had before in his life.

Frantically he worked at the knot around his wrists with his teeth. He had to get loose.

Bowen felt rough hands seize him and roll him from his hammock. It was Roger Three-Fingers, the bald, tattooed sail-maker, with two more of the crew. All had swords drawn.

"Be ye fer Morgan?" Three-Fingers demanded.

"Aye, Roger?" Bowen said, praying it was the right answer.

It didn't seem to be. With a growl, Three-Fingers shoved him harshly toward the hatch.

"Out on deck, boy!" he snarled. "Join Morgan and her friends!"

Bowen caught the rail. The ship pitched sud-

denly, and he pulled himself along toward the
main deck, where something seemed to be going on. Most of the crew had assembled
there—ringing Captain Morgan, Mr. Blair, Mr.
Glasspoole, and a couple of others. Morgan's
dagger was gone from the mast, replaced by
Scully's ax, he saw. Mutiny—that's what it
was.

He looked around wildly, but Roger Three-
Fingers gave him no chance to escape—and no
chance to help Morgan. He was thrust into the
center of the deck with the others.

A party of mutineers were putting the longboat over the side. With a crash, a wave swept
over all assembled, nearly swamping the deck.
Bowen fought to keep his feet.

Morgan, bracing herself, shouted: "If you
must have me dead, Mr. Scully, do it yourself!
Don't pretend I can survive in the storm!"

"I take no more orders from you!" Scully
shouted back. "I'm captain! Do any among you
wish to be her crew?"

Another wave swept over the side of the
ship. Bowen clung to a rope to keep his
feet.

"I'll row for her!" Mr. Glasspoole said, "and
God damn you forever, Tom Scully!"

Scully motioned, and Glasspoole was released. He went to join Morgan near where the
longboat was being launched. Several other
crewmen joined her as well, and they all
stared defiantly at Scully.

"Anyone else?" Scully bellowed. "Let him speak now!"

Blair stepped forward. "I prefer her company to yours, Tom Scully, and if we ever meet again, you won't leave with your head on your shoulders!"

Scully waved him over to Morgan and Glasspoole.

"Last call!" Scully said. "Who else—?"

Bowen edged forward cautiously. Scully wheeled on him.

"Where are you going, worm?" he bellowed.

"To be with my captain, you poxy-puking weasel!" Bowen bellowed back. He hurried over to Morgan.

"Save yourself, Mr. Bowen," Morgan whispered to him. "I doubt we'll make it."

"You need a strong oar—you don't have enough," he replied. Only a handful of others had crossed to stand with them.

"Tom Scully, the blood of these men is on your head!" Morgan said with finality. She climbed into the longboat first and was followed by Reed, then Glasspoole and the others, and lastly Bowen. The mutineers swung the boat out over the chopping, foaming waves, and then lowered it the rest of the way.

"At least give us a compass!" Morgan shouted up to Scully.

Scully threw back his head and laughed. "You're going nowhere but down!" he said.

With his cutlass he slashed the last tackle holding the boat, and it splashed freely into the waves.

Bowen looked desperately up at the *Morning Star*—and a sudden movement caught his eye. It was Dr. Shaw waving frantically from the poopdeck.

"Row, men!" Morgan cried, clinging to the tiller.

Everyone began unshipping the oars and locking them into place, and Bowen had no more time to worry about Shaw. He sat facing Captain Adams, took the oar, and began to pull with all his might.

"Morgan!" Shaw cried, despair filling him. He didn't give a farthing for his chances of staying alive with the other pirates here.

He glanced at the main deck and, to his horror, found Scully and the other mutineers staring straight at him.

"Somebody grab the doctor!" Scully shouted.

The longboat was just below him now, about to be swept away by the wind and waves. It turned. The men were rowing with all their might, turning their bow into the wind.

"I've followed you this far," he murmured.

Taking a deep breath, he dove into the water. He had always been a powerful swimmer, and he hoped he was up to the swim of his life.

He surfaced, wind whipping rain into his face, and turned slowly, riding up in the swell. Finally he spotted the longboat perhaps ten yards away. He tried to shout, but water filled his mouth and it came out as a choking gurgle.

Morgan sat in the box as coxswain. All the others were rowing as though their lives depended on it. They hadn't heard him, Shaw realized with dismay.

Swimming hard, he struck out for the long-boat. He had almost reached it when a wave, whipped up by a violent gust of wind, struck him in the face, knocking him back. To his dismay, he saw the boat begin to pull away. He waved his arms, bellowing for help, but it was no use. They pulled away from him rapidly, and then they were gone.

He saw something bobbing in the water next to him and grabbed at it out of desperation. It was a barrel—cargo from the *Morning Star* that had washed overboard, he realized. He clung to it desperately.

Bowen felt his muscles begin to ache, but he pulled with all his strength. Rain continued to pound down, harder than ever, and twenty-foot waves rose up on both sides of the little boat. They started up another swell—larger than any other they'd come to, Bowen thought—and he twisted around to see just as they reached the crest.

The longboat canted sharply downward, then slid forward into the trough like a runaway carriage. They hit the bottom hard, and water broke in over the rails.

"Put your backs into it!" Blair called.

Chastened, Bowen turned and began to row more strongly than ever. The wind whirled them about suddenly, and the longboat's bow turned to the side.

"Row hard!" Morgan cried. "It's our only hope!"

Bowen glanced to the side and saw an immense wave rising up before them. It was going to hit them broadside, he realized as it approached, climbing higher and higher before them.

"God help us all!" he cried.

The wave crashed over them. The longboat spun, and water sluiced across him with the force of a cannon's blast, ripping the oar from his hand. He felt himself being swept away and tried desperately to hang on.

Water surrounded him. Then he felt a hand on his collar, hauling him back to safety. It was Morgan, he realized a second later as the wave swept on.

She pulled him back to the longboat and, with Mr. Glasspoole's help, dragged him back aboard.

Sputtering, he found his oar and started rowing as hard as he could. There was nothing else he could do right now. This flimsy little boat was their only hope of salvation.

Morgan turned to them all, with a wall of water and lightning behind her. Her eyes were wild, and he saw the rage in every inch of her body.

"We must keep her bow to the waves!" Morgan said. "Row now, if you ever rowed in your life! Stretch your backs and burst your hearts! *Row, men, row!*"

Bowen felt something scrape along the bottom of the boat, sounding like an ax trying to cut through. He looked up at Morgan, panicked. Others had felt it, too, he saw—oars clashed as everyone lost the rhythm of their strokes, and the boat spun like a cork.

Blair, forward at the stroke oar, glanced over his shoulder at what they were approaching.

"White water ahead!" he screamed. "We're on a reef!"

Bowen half rose in his seat to see. Everyone else was doing the same.

"Stay with the boat!" Morgan screamed. "Stay with it—"

A huge wave shoved them up into the air, riding high. Then it threw them violently down. The boat's keel hit coral hard—and with a splintering sound, the keel snapped.

Bowen felt himself jolted from his seat. He went flying into the water along with everyone else. He had a glimpse of the boat breaking like a matchstick, and then another wave swept over everything and he was fighting to keep his head above water.

15

A loose oar struck Morgan in the shoulder as the longboat floundered and broke apart, and she managed to catch it and hang on. The wave dragged her over sharp coral, cutting her arms and legs, and then into rough, choppy water. Lightning flashed, thunder boomed like a cannon, rain slanted down, and over it all the constant roar of distant surf.

Kicking, holding on to the oar to keep her head above water, she tried to follow the sound of waves hitting shore. At first the sound would seem to get nearer; then a wave would catch her, swamp her completely, and pull her back. Only the oar buoying her up kept her from drowning, she thought.

The cold of the water ate into her, numbing her fingers and toes. Water filled her nose and mouth as she gasped for air. But still she struggled. She remembered her promise to her father. She remembered Dawg's leering face. But mostly she remembered Scully stealing the ship that was her birthright. It kept her going when a lesser person would have given up and slipped under the waves to a quiet, peaceful death.

After what seemed centuries, though, the rain began to slacken. It no longer fell in sheets, but pattered down like a jungle shower. The wind still gusted, but it had changed direction and the waves began to quiet, no longer topped by whitecaps.

Was that the beach ahead of her? With the last of her strength, she began to kick in that direction. And suddenly she found herself in a quieter lagoon, sheltered from the wind and the worst of the waves. More flotsam driven there by the storm floated nearby, and Morgan pulled herself onto a larger piece of what had once been the longboat.

She clung there, just hanging on, weak with exhaustion and lack of sleep, half drowsing.

When next she looked up, dawn had begun to brighten the east. The dark storm clouds had broken, and fingers of pink and yellow touched the sky.

"Morgan!" a weak voice cried.

Morgan raised her head, groggy. It was

Glasspoole, floating on another piece of debris to her side.

"Glasspoole!" she cried. "Are you all right?" She spotted a couple of others, too, and added, "Bowen? Blair?"

"Yes, we're here," Blair said, but we've lost Ames and Hewitt."

A quiet settled over everyone. The sea rocked them gently into a new position. They had to be as exhausted as she was, Morgan thought—perhaps more so, since they'd been rowing for an hour before the longboat broke apart.

"Morgan! Look!" Glasspoole suddenly cried.

He was pointing behind her. Morgan turned, half dreading what she might find. But instead of Dawg's ship, he was pointing to an island . . . an island with a very familiar rock formation.

"The rock pillars," Morgan said, surprised and awed. "It's Cutthroat—it must be!" It was just like the depiction on her piece of the map.

"God bless us all," Glasspoole said, grinning.

Morgan paddled to the narrow beach, more determined than ever. She pulled herself up and onto the sand, gasping for breath, and the others followed.

She wasted no time. She pulled out her two pieces of map—miraculously, she hadn't lost them in the water—and placed them next to each other. There was a gap where the third piece went. A dotted line indicated a trail running off one of the edges.

"We must find this trail," she said. "We'll make for high ground and get our bearings."

The others nodded. Somehow they'd managed to keep their cutlasses. They checked them, then pulled themselves to their feet. Everyone was dragging, Morgan thought. They'd rest later, she told herself, once they'd found out all there was to find.

A small winding trail, more suitable for goats than humans, led up from the beach. Large jagged rocks, some topped by luxuriant green growth, rose on either side of them. The air steamed in the tropical heat.

Morgan pushed a lock of hair out of her eyes as she concentrated on keeping her footing. When they lost sight of the beach and the jungle closed in around them, she heard mysterious animal noises all around—chirpings, chitterings, screeches. It's just birds and monkeys, she told herself, nothing to worry about. She hoped.

The trail turned again, then approached a ridge through the thick trees. As they reached the top, they could see a ship's mast. They hurried into a clearing—and Morgan gave a low moan.

Below them sat the *Reaper*, moored in a lovely cove. Then she brightened. Next to the *Reaper* sat the *Morning Star* . . . her ship.

"The *Reaper*," Bowen breathed.

"And *Morning Star* as well," Morgan said hopefully. "She still swims."

"Dawg must have caught Scully when he bore up in the storm."

"That scoundrel must have made a deal with Dawg," she said. And for that, she added to herself, he would pay with his life.

Dawg Brown surveyed the *Morning Star* from his position on her poopdeck and allowed himself a thin smile. He'd found Cutthroat, and his part of the map showed the treasure's location. And to top it all off, he had the *Morning Star*. If only he had Morgan in chains, his triumph would be complete.

"Them's the lot, Captain," Scully called up to him.

Dawg looked down. The few on the *Morning Star* whom Scully had identified as too loyal to Morgan Adams had been manacled to a long chain by Bishop.

"Take them below," he said.

"You heard the captain," Scully yelled, turning smartly toward the line of prisoners. "Get them belowdecks! Move it!"

Dawg nodded; a promising one, that Scully. He'd have to find a place in his own crew for the fellow. He liked it when men jumped—and jumped enthusiastically—when he spoke.

The line of prisoners began to shuffle through the open hatch. They had a sullen, beaten, doomed look to them that Dawg also liked.

"A pity Morgan ain't among them," he said to Snelgrave, who stood at his right hand.

"Lost in the storm, without a doubt," Snelgrave said.

Nodding, Dawg pulled out his own piece of the map. Treasure first, regrets later. He motioned Scully and several of his own most trusted men over. They came at a run.

He showed them his piece of the map. "Since we're here, this is the only piece that matters," he said. "Spread out and search the island. Find me this cove and this cliff. I'll wait ashore."

"Aye, Captain," they all said, turning for one of the longboats.

Dawg tucked the map back into the pouch he wore around his neck.

"Find me someplace suitable for a camp!" he called after them.

Morgan and her men hunkered down in the clearing to watch Dawg's men come ashore. From under the cover of trees, Morgan had little fear that Dawg or his men would spot them. She just wished she still had her spyglass.

One of the longboats began to row toward shore. She could see Scully and half a dozen of Dawg's men inside. Scully seemed to fit right in with them, she thought, scum with scum.

"He makes to go ashore," she said. "We'll follow him, get the map, and find the treasure."

Rising, she drew her cutlass and, using it like a machete, began to hack a path through the jungle growth. The others did the same.

Shaw had always been an excellent thief. He'd always prided himself on his skill, his ability to think on his feet, his stealth, and his brash daring. He'd gotten into places like the Governor's Ball in Jamaica because he'd dared what few other thieves had dared.

He'd clung to his barrel through the storm, alternately praying and paddling, and he'd wound up here, in this cove. Fortunately he'd had the good sense to crawl up from the beach and into the trees well before dawn; the wind, rain, and waves had hidden his tracks. When the two ships had pulled in at dawn, he had watched from a safe vantage point.

One was the *Morning Star*; the other had to be Dawg Brown's ship. For once he was glad he hadn't stayed aboard the night before. Everything happens for a reason, he told himself, and he'd been swept here alone because he was meant to have the treasure for himself.

Secure with that thought, he drew back a little farther into the grass. The pirates were lowering a longboat, he saw. Probably sending scouts ashore. They wouldn't see him where he lay, he knew; it would be a matter of biding his time. He could be a very patient man when he had to be.

Slowly he reached down, pulled off his boots, and laid them out to dry. No sense wasting his wait, he thought.

Throughout the day he periodically looked out on the pirates. They were setting up their camp about two hundred yards away, on the beach. What he'd first taken to be driftwood on the beach turned out to be bones—thousands of human bones, he thought—and they were using the bones like wood to construct lean-tos and huts, chairs and tables. They lit a huge campfire and began to roast birds and a small pig they'd killed, and Shaw found his mouth watering at the smell. His stomach rumbled.

Finally he saw Dawg Brown, looking fearsome as ever, come ashore in a longboat. Dawg made a quick tour of the camp and seemed to find it satisfactory. He sat at the table, drew a bit of paper from the pouch around his neck, and began to study it closely.

Shaw caught his breath. The map—that had to be the third piece. He wanted it. He had to have it. Later that night, he told himself, he'd make his attempt.

He eased back in the grass and felt his boots. Still damp, but much better than they'd been. He pulled them on. Things were definitely looking up, he thought. You couldn't steal something unless you knew where it was, and now that he knew where Dawg kept the map, everything had started to fall into place in his mind.

Morgan called a halt around noon, and everyone pretty much dropped where he'd been standing. Morgan leaned back against a tree. Her arms and legs felt like water, and her head pounded. She had been too long without sleep, she thought.

"We'll rest here for two hours," she said. "We'll take turns standing watch. I'll go first, then Mr. Glasspoole, Mr. Bowen, and Mr. Blair. Sleep while you can. You'll need it later."

Gratefully, everyone curled up. Soon they were snoring.

Morgan forced herself to her feet, listening above the cries of birds for any sounds of Dawg's men. She heard nothing unusual. They were probably still on the beach setting up camp, she thought.

They'd have to pay Dawg a visit that night . . .

Shaw watched throughout the rest of the day, chewing on stalks of grass to try to alleviate his hunger. Dawg Brown, he noticed, had selected the largest hut at the center of the camp. As evening wore on and dusk deepened toward night, the pirates gorged on island food, drank themselves into a stupor, and collapsed one by one. Stretching and yawning, Dawg Brown retreated into his bone hut. He still had the pouch around his neck.

I bet he sleeps with a knife in each hand, Shaw thought with a shiver. This was going to be the most dangerous stunt of his life.

He counted to a hundred slowly, watching, waiting. None of the pirates moved. The campfire, slowly dying to embers, sent a flickering orange light through the cove.

Slowly, carefully, Shaw eased himself forward. He stood, feeling the sand beneath his feet, straining to hear. A few stray birds still cooed from the jungle, and the waves lapped softly at the beach, but that was it.

He crept forward a step at a time, cringing as the sand crunched too loudly beneath his boots. Pausing, he slipped them off and tied them to his belt. Barefoot, he moved forward again, this time as silently as a ghost.

He passed several sleeping crewmen, their heads pillowed on their arms. One of them he recognized as Scully, and for an instant he allowed his thoughts to turn to vengeance. It would be so easy to slit Scully's throat while he slept . . . but then he shook his head. He was a thief, not a murderer, and more than revenge he wanted money—the treasure Dawg's map showed, to be precise.

Creeping forward again, he approached Dawg's hut. Low snores sounded inside. Perfect, he thought.

Kneeling, he continued into the hut on hands and knees. It took his eyes a few seconds to adjust to the dimness inside. The pouch still hung around Dawg's neck.

Slowly Shaw drew his knife and eased the tip up over Dawg's side, angling it toward Dawg's neck. His hand followed. Slowly he slipped the knife under the leather thong holding the map pouch, and his fingers gently gripped the pouch for support.

He snipped it, then lifted the pouch away. Easiest job he'd ever done.

But it wasn't over yet. Slowly he began to creep backward out of the hut.

Dawg Brown felt a light touch on his chest and stilled his breathing. With one hand, he reached for his knife.

Cautiously, he opened his eyes. It wasn't a hand, but a spider he saw. Casually he crushed it, then rolled onto his side and felt for his map.

It was gone.

With a roar of rage, he leapt to his feet and darted outside. There—what was that shape slinking off in the dark?

He pulled his pistol and fired. Half drunk, the pirates around him were rousing from their sleep. Several fired pistols as well, but the shape ducked and vanished from sight.

"Morgan's here!" Dawg screamed. "The infernal trollop has stolen my map—"

* * *

Morgan, watching the sudden commotion in Dawg's camp, could scarcely believe her ears when Dawg began bellowing that she had stolen his map. She strained to see and saw someone who looked like Shaw fleeing into the jungle.

Dawg was raging through the camp with his cutlass drawn. "She's here and you let her in, damn you all!" he was bellowing. "Find her or not one of you stays alive!"

His men scattered into the jungle like scared rabbits. Several of them were headed toward the spot where Morgan and her men crouched.

Morgan let the branch fall back, hiding them from the camp. "Shaw . . ." she whispered. Strangely, she felt relieved rather than angered. That puzzled her.

"He's alive," Bowen said.

"More lives than an alley cat," Morgan said. "And they'll catch him—the blockhead. Spread out—if he makes it this far, we'll grab him."

Dawg's men quickly made torches and set out after Shaw. There were at least fifty of them, Morgan estimated, combing the jungle in bands of twos and threes.

And Shaw was leading them right to her.

Motioning to Bowen, Blair, and Glasspoole to follow her, she set off after him herself.

"Morgan!" she heard Dawg calling. "Morgan, come out! You know it's only a matter of time before I find you!"

If he found her, Morgan vowed to herself, she would be the last thing he saw.

She glimpsed Shaw twenty yards away and plunged after him, her men at her heels, but he heard her coming and bolted like a scared rabbit. Then there were torches ahead—Dawg's men!—and she had to double back, crouching low to avoid being seen.

"Down!" she whispered, and everyone stayed crouched motionless. A troop of Dawg's men ran past. Then the coast was clear, and she motioned everyone on.

Dawg's men seemed to be concentrating far to the left. They hadn't seen Shaw, she realized . . . but she had.

"Shaw!" she called softly. "Shaw, where are you, damn you?"

Glasspoole held up his hand for silence. They stopped and listened. Far off, but very faintly, they heard a voice—

"Help!"

"This way," Morgan said, setting out. She used her cutlass like a machete again, and soon opened a path to a small clearing.

Only a few feet away, in the center of the clearing, Shaw was up to his knees in quicksand and sinking fast.

"You want to be careful," he whispered to her. "It's quicksand."

"You bastard," Morgan whispered back. "Did you get Dawg's map?"

He held up the pouch Dawg had worn around his neck.

"Hand it over or you're a dead man," she said.

"Did you ever think I might have taken it to bring to you?"

"Not for one second," Morgan said. "Up to your knees and sinking, you can still do nothing but lie."

"No, ma'am," he said very sincerely, "it's completely true. I could no longer stand your opinion of me . . ."

"Then give it over, you weasel."

"I will, at once, with all my heart—if you'd be so good as to get me out first."

"You think I was born Wednesday? Give it here—then we'll talk of rescue."

"I, of course, see your point of view—but for me, it works better if I'm first on the hard part of the land."

He was still sinking fast. "You're up to your waist," Morgan pointed out.

Shaw looked down. "But you see," he said quickly, "given how we've been up to now, the two of us, I must think, What if I give it to you and you leave me here? It wasn't long ago that you spoke of marooning me . . ."

"What if I pull you out and you swallow it, or hide it, or run away? You're beyond trusting."

"It keeps coming back to trust, don't it?" He gave her a quick grin. Then he looked down. He was up to his chest. "That's the trouble with being a cheat," he went on. "Nobody knows when you're telling the truth. I was after your treasure, I admit it, I was out to screw you from the beginning—but that word has two meanings, don't it, and the more I followed the first, the more and more I thought of the second. You became better to me than gold."

Morgan eyed him. He'd soon be in over his head, and then she'd have lost the map. But could she believe anything of what he said? Truly she felt for him.

She glanced to the right. Dawg's men were returning. She could see the flicker of torches through the trees.

"Give me your sword tip," Shaw said urgently.

"What for?" she asked suspiciously.

"Do it—don't argue—"

Holding on to Blair, Morgan leaned out over the quicksand with her cutlass toward Shaw. He pulled Dawg's map from the pouch and stuck it on the tip of the sword, where it fluttered faintly.

"There—it's no valentine, but it will have to do. Now you have it all and I have nothing. I'm at your mercy, Morgan—do with me whatever you want."

No man had ever said that to Morgan before. She found herself softening inside. God, she hated him—and yet she found something irresistible, something charming, about him. She looked at the last piece of the map, finally in her hand.

"Oh, fish him out," she said. She turned away so nobody would see the tears in her eyes.

Blair whacked off a hanging tree vine and tossed it out to Shaw. He gratefully grabbed hold, and the three men pulled him to safety.

16

It took them the rest of the night to elude Dawg's men. Dawn found Morgan and her crew exhausted and filthy, but safe on the far side of the island.

The five of them knelt on a lagoon beach against a tropical sunrise. Despite all the trouble and hardships, this had to be one of the happiest days of her life, Morgan thought.

She put Harry's scalp map down on the sand, then took out Mordechai's map and joined the two. Lastly she took out Dawg's piece of the map and set it in place.

Together they formed a large X in the center of the island.

"There's our treasure," Morgan announced proudly.

"Let's go get it!" Bowen cried, and everyone gave a cheer.

Morgan scooped up the pieces, turned, and stared up at the rocky center of the island. "This way," she said, striking out.

The map brought her to the top of a rocky cliff.

"Here," she said to Shaw, handing him Dawg's piece again. "More words in that Latin writing. What does it say?"

"Seventy-five paces north from the rock column," he read.

Morgan spotted the rock easily enough: a tall spike of stone jutting up. She ran to it, found her bearings, and turned north.

"One . . . two . . . three," she began counting, pacing due north. "Eighteen . . . nineteen—"

She suddenly looked up to nothing but blue ahead, sky and sea. She had come to the edge of a treacherous cliff. Sharp rocks lay at the bottom of a hundred-and-fifty-foot drop. Glasspoole steadied her elbow to keep her from falling.

"Seventy-five?" she asked Shaw, turning to look at him.

"That's what it says," he replied. He studied the map again nevertheless.

"You misread it," Morgan said half accusingly.

"No, it's clear—seventy-five paces from the rock column."

"Then the last fifty are out there," she said,

turning to gaze out across the water. Had the cliff given way and fallen since the treasure was buried? Shores changed; it had been a long time since the map was made.

"What now?" Bowen asked.

"Down we go." She indicated the craggy rocks far below, where waves crashed and foamed.

They spent an hour making crude ropes from vines, then returned to the cliff. Glasspoole and Blair secured the ends of the two ropes to tree trunks while Morgan tied one end around her waist. Blair then made to tie himself to the other.

"Let Mr. Shaw try it," Morgan told him. "If the rope breaks, what have we lost?"

Shaw laughed as if she'd made a joke, but quickly tied the other end around his waist. Morgan gave a nod and Glasspoole, Blair, and Bowen began lowering them down the cliff face.

"Be careful here," Shaw said as they were twenty feet over the edge.

"Careful yourself," Morgan said. "I grew up climbing shroud lines."

"I once climbed the Matterhorn in a blizzard," he boasted. Morgan shot him a disbelieving look, and he quickly added, "I did, I swear it—there are some things I've actually done."

They descended another thirty feet, and

then below an overhang Morgan found herself staring into the mouth of a cave. She felt her heart begin to pound. Nineteen feet to the edge of the cliff . . . then about another sixty down . . . that could be the seventy-five feet the map spoke of!

She cupped her hands to her mouth and shouted up, "We found a cave in the cliff!"

They lowered her another few feet, and swinging her body on the rope, Morgan rocked her way into the cave mouth. She released herself and dropped, looking around with interest.

Behind her, she heard Shaw hit the floor with a low "Oof."

Stalactites hung from the ceiling; stalagmites rose to meet them. Somewhere in the darkness, water dripped, and a wet, dank smell came forth.

"This seems promising," Morgan said.

"It does?" Shaw asked, joining her. She saw him shiver a bit; he looked distinctly uneasy here.

"What does the map say?" she asked.

He pulled it out and read, "Go where your feet cannot take you." He traded a puzzled look with her.

"Come on," Morgan said, leading the way deeper.

The cave twisted a bit, then opened up into an underground lake. Across from them, in the center of the lake, lay what looked like a small island.

"We're getting closer!" Shaw said, sounding excited. It was amazing how quickly his fears melted away at the thought of money, Morgan thought.

She waded into the water and swam with strong, even strokes. He joined her. When they reached the island, they climbed out and stood for a minute looking around them. A path led deeper into the little rocky island.

Morgan followed it, with Shaw right on her heels. Rounding a corner, she came face-to-face with a man and drew back suddenly. Shaw bumped into her.

It wasn't a man, she realized suddenly; it was only a skull . . . sitting on top of a pile of skulls. There were hundreds of them.

"Harry, I found it!" she breathed.

"Where?" Shaw asked, looking around.

Morgan looked, too, but didn't see anything but the skulls. Dripping water echoed off the cranium of one. There wasn't anything else; the trail came to an end here.

Or did it? Morgan stuck her toe into the pile. They rustled—loose. Growing excited, she bent and began pulling the skulls apart, shoving them this way and that.

"Bear a hand," she said to Shaw.

He did, with visible reluctance. Then they both saw something gleaming underneath, and suddenly it was a free-for-all, with both of them scrambling to knock skull after skull aside. It was a rotted chest, Morgan realized as they unearthed it—covered with rotting spiderwebs and patina. As more skulls began to roll free, she saw more chests, and behind them, a five-foot-tall golden crucifix. Her heart bounded and her breath came short; she could hardly believe her eyes.

Grabbing the handle of one small chest that still seemed intact, Morgan dragged it free of the pile and scrubbed off the top. Copper gleamed brilliantly beneath it. She undid the clasp, lifted the lid, and found inside the dried and desiccated bodies of hundreds of beetles and spiders, the filth of many years. But among it . . . among it gleamed hundreds if not thousands of gold coins, diamonds, and loose precious stones.

Shaw hugged her with joy, and she was so amazed she forgot to stop him.

They quickly dug out the other chests and opened them. They contained a vast array of gold, silver, and stunning gems and jewelry. It was more than a king's ransom, Morgan thought. It was gold enough to buy an empire.

"We'd best get these out," she said. "Dawg can't be far behind."

"Fetch the others," Shaw said. "I'll start hauling these to the entrance."

Morgan nodded, then caught herself. Shaw hadn't proved himself that much to her—what would he do with the treasure once he was alone with it?

He seemed to sense her thoughts. "Morgan,

that's unworthy," he told her. "What could I do—steal all this, take your ship back from Dawg, and sail it away all by myself?"

"Cut a deal with him," she said.

"Morgan . . ."

"All right, I'm going," she said. "But no tricks. And hurry!"

Turning, she sprinted to the lake, climbed into one of the canoes, and pushed off. When she glanced over her shoulder, she found Shaw dragging the first of the chests down to the shore.

Nodding, she continued to paddle.

Glasspoole leaned forward and gazed down the face of the cliff to where the vine ropes vanished. Morgan and Shaw had been gone quite a while, and he'd begun to have an uneasy feeling inside. Had that thieving doctor done something to her? He had half a mind to go after them himself to see what had happened.

"Mr. Glasspoole!" Blair suddenly said.

Glasspoole turned. Blair was holding up his hand, and Glasspoole strained to hear.

Not far away, the sounds of Dawg's men beating through the undergrowth reached him.

"If they catch us here, they'll find Morgan and the treasure," Blair said.

Glasspoole said, "We cannot risk it."

"This way," Blair said, heading off into the trees. Glasspoole hesitated half a second, then followed. Dawg's men had to come first, he thought. They were the biggest and most immediate threat.

Morgan reached the mouth of the cave and tugged hard on one of the ropes. There should have followed an answering tug, or at least a shout, but she heard and felt nothing. Puzzled, she leaned out as far as she dared.

"Mr. Blair? Mr. Glasspoole?" she shouted. "Can you hear me?"

No answer reached her. A stray gull cawed far below. Puzzled, wondering what could have gone wrong, Morgan took the rope in hand, swung out away from the cave mouth, and began to climb up the side of the cliff.

She was panting for breath when she reached the top and levered herself over the edge. The little cleared area was completely empty. She saw not a trace of Blair, Bowen, or Glasspoole. Where had they gone?

Pausing, she listened for a moment, but heard nothing. She headed off for the trees. Remembering the rays of light slanting down from the roof of the cave, she wondered if they'd found another way down.

She entered the darkness of the jungle growth, still listening for trouble. "Mr. Blair?" she called. "Mr. Glasspoole?"

She heard a clank behind her and froze in place. It had been a sound of metal grating against metal . . . a very *familiar* sound.

She wheeled—and found herself face-to-face

with Snelgrave. He grinned and hefted the chain at the end of his wrist, and it clinked again, louder than before.

"Morgan," he breathed, "lucky me. We was looking all over for you."

Morgan tried to run, but Dawg's men swarmed at her from all around. It had been a trap, she realized. She began to struggle—but to no avail. They had her arms in grips that couldn't be broken.

17

They hauled her to another jungle clearing, where Morgan was dismayed to find Glasspoole, Blair, and Bowen and her other men standing prisoner. Their hands were tied, and they looked like they'd been severely beaten—they hadn't given up without a fight, at least.

Snelgrave and Bishop tied her by her wrists between two trees. Dawg wandered over to watch with interest as Bishop, with no warning or ceremony, abruptly ripped down her shirt, exposing her breasts. Dawg and most of his men began to grin. Morgan glared defiantly. She wouldn't give him the pleasure of resisting . . . yet.

"Worth waiting for, Morgan," Dawg said. "A

highlight of my life." Handing his dagger to Snelgrave, he strode toward her. "You're muddy," he went on. "I reckon you've been digging. Say where and I won't bury or slice you or anything else that might cross my mind."

In response, Morgan pulled up her knees and gave Snelgrave a mighty kick to the stomach. Doubling over, he reeled away from her.

"Ah, Morgan," Dawg said with mock sympathy. "Brave to the last, but unfortunately it won't do you any good." He motioned to Snelgrave. "When you're ready, Mr. Snelgrave."

Snelgrave struggled upright, then with a grin circled around behind her. Morgan twisted, trying to see what he was up to—but she needn't have bothered: she felt the cut when he sliced her back—cleanly, but not deeply, she thought with a gasp. It hurt, but it could have hurt a lot more. It seemed they intended to draw out her torture.

Snelgrave made another cut, then another. He was breathing hard, enjoying the work, Morgan thought.

"The notion of killing every last one of my living relatives closes a certain circle, if you get my meaning," Dawg said.

Snelgrave made two more cuts in quick succession. Morgan squirmed, but refused to cry out. She knew that was what her uncle wanted. And it was the last thing she'd give him now. Neither that nor the location of the treasure.

Dawg leaned forward and studied her face acutely. "Ain't had enough yet? Well . . ." He turned and picked up a bucket. It was filled with bread, Morgan saw. "My men donated their bread ration," he went on. "Wasn't that fine of them?"

He pulled the bread off the top, revealing a slithering, squirming, crawling mass of maggots and other wriggling bugs. Morgan had to turn her head away.

He held it closer. It was a gruesome, frightening sight.

"A fact about maggots," Dawg said. "There's only one thing they prefer to bread." He circled her, raising the bucket. "And that's meat . . . red, raw, bloody meat."

Morgan felt a terror like none she'd ever experienced sweep through her. It was inhuman . . . monstrous. She tried to break free, to squirm away from the bucket.

"People who know tell me the most painful feeling in the world is a maggot crawling into an open wound. They eat and eat—they eventually chew into your spine, and then you die. That takes time, and until then . . . exquisite pain."

He tipped the bucket toward her back. The maggots crawled hungrily up the side toward her flayed skin. He tilted it more, and first one then another maggot spilled out.

"So which will it be, Morgan?" he asked

softly. "Treasure—or the sound of little mouths feeding?"

Morgan pressed her eyes closed and shook her head. She couldn't tell him. God save her, she couldn't!

"Here come the first," Dawg said. "I assume they're calling the good news to their friends, in little maggot happiness."

"Give me a sword, Uncle—or are you afraid to fight me?"

"Almost exactly what your father said," Dawg replied. "You remind me of him—the part of you that's about to die, I mean."

He tipped the bucket farther. More maggots slid onto Morgan's back. She felt their mouths latching on, biting. She pressed her eyes shut, trying to will herself dead or away.

Suddenly, from somewhere, came a familiar voice.

"Dawg Brown?" Shaw's voice called. "Unless I'm very wrong, I have something that would please you greatly."

Morgan opened her eyes in surprise, the pain of the maggots forgotten. Shaw stood off at the far edge of the clearing among the trees. Dawg stared at him.

"That one again," he said suddenly. "Somebody shoot him."

Half a dozen men fired at once, and Shaw dropped out of sight into the undergrowth.

"Find the body!" he snarled, and more of his

men hurried over to the spot where Shaw had been.

"He ain't here!" one of them called.

"Find him!" Turning, he clobbered Morgan in the side of the head with his fist, and she slumped against the ropes, stunned.

She was barely aware of his brushing the maggots back into the bucket and cutting her free. Then, retrieving his knife from Snelgrave, he dragged her after him, heading for the spot where Shaw had been. Morgan let herself stumble after him. If she was going to get a chance to escape, it would be now, she realized distantly.

Ahead, Dawg's men shouted and gave chase. They'd spotted Shaw, Morgan realized, close to tears. Dawg and Snelgrave followed.

They came out onto the edge of the cliff where the map had led them. Dawg drew up short and looked at his men, who seemed bewildered.

"Where'd he go?" Bishop demanded.

"Look over the cliff, Mr. Brown!" a weak voice called.

Dawg stepped to the edge and looked down. Morgan, beside him, could see Shaw hanging precariously on one of the two ropes—and tied alongside him, on the other rope, dangled one of the treasure chests.

"It's the pretty man from Spittalfield. What have you got there?" Dawg demanded.

Shaw held a knife against the rope to which

the chest was tied. If he cut it, Morgan saw, the chest would fall—and its contents would be lost forever on the rocks below.

"Treasure," Shaw said. "Bags of it. Be careful what you do—you have much to lose."

Dawg leaned back and said to Snelgrave, "Can you put a ball between his eyes?"

"You'd say good-bye to four million pounds," Shaw called up. "That's a guess, but I can't be off more than a million or so."

"Cut the rope, William!" Morgan suddenly called. "Get away!"

Dawg hauled her back from the cliff's edge and shook her savagely. "Well, William," he said, "let's make a deal. I've been known to be reasonable."

"Send Morgan down," he called.

"Don't be a fool, William!" Morgan called. "He'll kill us anyway!"

"I'll send the treasure up and we'll both have what we want!"

"Who is this fellow?" Dawg asked Morgan. "Your shining knight? Your Romeo?" He looked at Snelgrave. "I believe we're looking at love, Mr. Snelgrave!"

Then he leaned forward. "Very well—we have a deal," he said. "Here she comes."

Putting his hand on her back, Dawg shoved Morgan over the edge. Screaming, she fell like a stone. She found herself rushing at the rocks and Shaw faster than she would have thought possible.

Shaw suddenly shoved himself off the cliff with his feet. Swinging out as far on the rope as he could, he reached for her—and caught her. Their hands locked on each other's wrists, and then they went swinging wildly on the end of the rope.

On the clifftop above them, Dawg laughed. "Now we have both," Morgan heard him say. "Haul them in."

His men began to pull them up. Shaw clung tightly to Morgan, his face ashen.

"I confess I'm at a loss as to what to do now," he said.

Dawg called down, "Come to me, Morgan!"

"Let me go," Morgan said. At least it would be a clean, fast death, she thought.

"I won't," William Shaw said. "Not for the world!"

"Please," she said. "It's much kinder than what waits for me up there."

"And what about me?"

"There's some chance Dawg won't bother to kill you, and it's better than the alternative."

"Which is . . . ?"

"Burial at sea."

"I wish I'd never learnt Latin," he said bitterly.

"Don't watch me fall," Morgan said.

"I'm coming with you!"

"Don't be mad. Why?"

"I guess I'm falling for you."

"I can't let—" Morgan began.

"Don't argue," he said. "Let us, for once, agree on something."

He really meant it, Morgan thought. The look in his eyes told her that much.

"Thank you," Morgan said. "On the count of three, then. One . . . two . . ."

"Wait!" Shaw said. "One more thing."

"What?"

"Considering everything, I really think that from now on we should be partners . . . full partners. What do you say?"

Morgan paused. "Sixty-forty."

"Equal. Fifty-fifty."

"Right, then," she said. "Shall we shake on it?"

Shaw grinned, and she knew he understood the joke. They both laughed one last time.

"Ready now?" Morgan said.

"I'm ready," he said somberly.

Morgan looked down. "One . . ." she said.

"Look at me!"

"Two . . ."

"Morgan," he said, "I want to be looking in your eyes—"

"Shh!" she said. Maybe there was a chance, she thought, studying the waves rolling in.

William looked hurt. "Just trying to be romantic," he said.

"Look, watch there," she said.

"Watch what?"

She pointed down past their feet, counting to herself. "Twelve . . . thirteen—the wave!"

Shaw began to nod; she knew he saw the massive wave crashing over the rocks below and rushing out again. It covered the rocks for the briefest of moments.

"There's a swell every thirteen seconds," she said. "How long will it take us to fall? Three?"

"I guess four," he said.

"Then hold me tight and let go of the rope on the nine count. One . . . two . . ."

They were almost to the top. Dawg was grinning down at them.

"Come to me, dear Morgan," he said, reaching for her. "I will bounce you on my knee again."

"Six . . . seven . . . eight . . . now!" she cried.

Shaw let go. They both plummeted together with nothing but rocks below.

18

*R*eed, lost in thoughts, had taken a stroll along the beach to try to reconcile himself to Morgan's death. Dawg's tale of her plunge to the rocks while in Shaw's arms had a certain dark poetry, he thought. "Love—who can explain it?" had been Dawg's comment.

Then he saw a body lying half in the surf. He sprinted over to it, turned it over, and recognized William Shaw.

"Shaw! Shaw!" he said. If he was alive—what about Morgan?

Shaw stumbled to his feet, staring wildly out to sea.

"Morgan—have you seen Morgan—?" Shaw gasped.

Reed paused. Dawg and Ainslee might like this one back, he thought. If Morgan hadn't lived through the fall, he'd make sure Shaw didn't either.

"Yes, I did." he lied. "I helped her ashore— and then I saw you."

"She's alive," Shaw said, relief flooding through him. His knees felt weak and he almost collapsed. "Thank God! Where is she?"

"Where Dawg can't find her," Reed said. "Come with me."

He turned and started walking up the beach quickly, and after a few more deep breaths, he heard Shaw follow.

Reed glanced back, saw how slowly Shaw was moving, and jogged back. Then, running backward, he kept pace with him.

"How'd you get off the ship?" Shaw asked.

"Same as you," Reed said. "I jumped. Fortunately, I'm an excellent swimmer. Ah, yes—up here, if you please, Mr. Shaw." He turned away from the beach and headed into the jungle.

"This seems very far from the beach," Shaw said doubtfully.

Then, as he pushed back a branch and stepped into a clearing, he drew up short. Before him, seated at a table on the shore of the lagoon, were Governor Ainslee, Trotter, Dawg Brown, several of Dawg's men, and a line of armed redcoats. Ainslee and Dawg had cups of tea in front of them.

Panicked, he looked up at Ainslee.

"Mr. Shaw—you survived after all," the governor said, "and just in time to witness an historic alliance in the making."

"And Morgan?" Dawg called.

"There was no sign of her anywhere," Reed said. "I don't think she made it."

"No doubt," Ainslee said, "you are wondering how I wound up here. A little bird told me, courtesy of our Mr. Reed."

Shaw glared at Reed, who backed away guiltily.

"You double-crossing bastard!" Shaw said. With the last of his strength, Shaw whirled and clobbered Reed. That was for lying to him, he thought. That was for betraying Morgan. And most of all it was for luring him away while he still might have found and saved her.

Half a dozen redcoats piled on top of Shaw, grabbing his arms and legs when he tried to punch and kick.

Dawg Brown watched as Shaw was quickly knocked unconscious. Good, he thought. One less gnat whining in his ear.

He turned to Ainslee. "A word alone, Governor?" he said.

Ainslee motioned to his men, who stepped back. "So," Ainslee said, "are my terms agreeable to you?"

"A Royal Pardon?" Dawg asked.

"My word as a gentleman."

"But I still rape, steal, and kill."

"As a Privateer for England? Of course. As long as they're Spanish."

"Of course. It's time I mend my ways." He turned to Bishop. "Rum!"

Bishop brought him a bottle. He uncorked it and poured a liberal dose into Ainslee's teacup, then raises the bottle in a toast.

"Your health," he said.

Stunned from the fall, Morgan Adams felt the undertow pull her down toward the ocean floor. She knew she had to act fast or she'd be pulled a mile or more out to sea by the powerful current.

She whipped her legs up under her and, with the last of her strength, kicked away from the ocean floor. The push broke her free of the current, and she saw the shimmer of sun on waves overhead. Struggling, she managed to reach the surface. There she gasped, too weak to do more than tread water and try to catch her breath.

She was a hundred yards out from shore, well to the side of the cliff where she and Shaw had jumped. Shaw—where was he? Had the current taken him, too?

"William?" she tried to call, but she choked and all that came out was a cough. No man had ever wanted to die for her before If anything had happened to him—if he hadn't made it, too—she didn't know what she'd do.

Slowly, painfully, she struck back for shore.

The swim seemed to take hours, and the rocks remained annoyingly far away. Finally, though, she felt loose sand and gravel shifting under her feet and half stood, half dragged herself the rest of the way ashore.

She lay in the shallows, panting, feeling her heart pound as though it would burst. "William—" she called softly. "Where are you—?"

Finally she found she had strength enough to stand once more. Carefully she picked her way along the shore, through the rocks, toward the beach on the far side of the cliff.

A man's laugh brought her up short. Who could that be?

Crouching, she crept forward to see. On the beach, two hundred yards away, she saw a line of redcoats . . . and at its head, the richly dressed man who had chased her in Jamaica, Governor Ainslee. Behind them they were dragging a very bedraggled-looking prisoner . . . William Shaw!

Relief swept over her, then anger, then dread. Someone had betrayed her. And she had a suspicion she knew just who that someone had been.

19

Numb inside and out, William Shaw stared up at Ainslee, Trotter, Dawg Brown, Snelgrave, Bishop, and several royal marines through slitted eyes. They were in a longboat rowing out to the three ships in the cove: the *Morning Star*, the *Reaper*, and two British Men-of-War. The ships were anchored side by side.

Shaw lay in chains; around him sat treasure chests taken from the hidden cave, laden with a fortune in gold and jewels. Between them, the pirates and Ainslee's redcoats had wasted no time in bringing it all out.

Ainslee and Dawg both seemed ebullient.

"Discretion dictates I return my share to

Port Royal on a neutral vessel, rather than a navy ship. You don't have much feel for these things, Trotter. You will in time."

"I hope so, sir," Trotter said.

The longboat came alongside Ainslee's ship. "Get a message to Captain Perkins to set sail," Ainslee went on. "We'll follow in a few hours' time."

"Very well, sir," Trotter said, rising. Shaw watched him climb up the rope ladder to the deck.

Several of the pirates dragged Shaw up the side to the deck, and then they began moving the treasure aboard in slings. Dawg and Ainslee stood together watching it being lowered into the hold through an open cargo hatch in the deck.

"Take a few of the men and follow us in the *Morning Star*," Ainslee said. "You'll get a share of her sale price. A little here, a little there—it adds up."

Trotter beamed. "Thank you, sir—I daresay!"

Ainslee turned to Dawg. "And now you, sir—it must spoil your pleasure a bit, me here and horning in on your treasure, but *asi es la vida*. I'm a man of my word, however. I shall go right now to write your royal pardon and letter of marque. You shall have it within the hour. You'll find privateering for the Crown to be so much more profitable."

Nodding and smiling to himself, Ainslee headed aft.

Snelgrave leaned close to Dawg. Shaw had to strain to hear.

"Why do you let that preening swab live?" he asked in a low voice.

"I study him," Dawg said. "When I become governor of Jamaica, I will want some of his manners."

Shaw swallowed. Dawg Adams as governor of Jamaica—the thought appalled him. And yet, somehow, he could see it happening.

The taking of treasure, Lieutenant Trotter reflected on his fifth trip from the shore to the *Morning Star* with a full longboat, rapidly descended to the tedious. He glanced down at those seated in the boat with him . . . Glasspoole and Blair, their names were. With bound hands, no weapons, and a swift hanging waiting for them back in Jamaica, they had little to live for. Their sullen expressions and unhappy eyes spoke volumes.

Scully, who was captaining the *Morning Star*—for the moment, anyway, Trotter thought—leaned over to watch their progress.

"Get them aboard," Trotter told his men, and they began bundling Glasspoole and Blair onto the deck.

Trotter nimbly climbed the rope ladder hanging over the side. "Lock them below with the others," he told Scully. "They all hang at Port Royal."

"With pleasure, your honor."

Scully turned and shouted instructions to his crew. They, and the redcoats who formed the prize crew, hurried to obey. The longboat was quickly raised, and sails were loosed from the yardarms.

"Weigh anchor—rouse the watch forward!" Scully called. He seemed to know what he was doing, Trotter thought with a measure of satisfaction. He hoped for a fast and uneventful journey home.

On the forecastle above, the men heaved the capstan around. As the anchor broke water, sails were lowered into place. The canvas snapped out and filled with wind, and the ship began to move.

Trotter nodded happily. He turned to look back at the island, then out toward the British Man-of-War they were following. A quick and uneventful trip, he thought . . . and plenty of gold waiting at its end.

Morgan had always been an excellent swimmer. But swimming to civilization from Cutthroat Island was beyond even her most daring thoughts. When she saw the *Morning Star* being loaded with treasure and prisoners, she knew she had to be on board when it sailed.

Tom Scully seemed to be showing off his

newfound captaincy, but whether he was trying to impress the redcoats or his own crew she couldn't say. She *did* know he had everyone on board jumping, repairing storm damage, cleaning, polishing. Not one hand remained idle aboard ship.

It all worked to her advantage. Even the shore crew loading the longboat wasn't paying attention. They all thought her dead. Well, you could never count an Adams out until you saw the body personally, she thought.

She slipped into the water, took a deep breath, and dived down low, taking powerful strokes. The cove ran deep; the *Morning Star* sat close to shore. She made it to the hull just as her lungs felt like they would burst.

She broke surface, took a single deep breath, and ducked down again. Following the hull, she reached the stern and found the rudder. There she surfaced again, clinging to the anchor rope, trying to keep her breathing measured and quiet.

It took time, but eventually even her heartbeat returned to something near normal. She watched; she waited. The longboat rowed out, Scully took it aboard, and then she heard the crew going through preparations to set sail.

The anchor rope shifted and began to rise. Morgan let it slip through her fingers. As the anchor itself appeared, she took firm hold and let them pull her up out of the water on one of the flukes.

As the anchor neared the cathead, she slipped through an open gun port and into the ship. There she paused, balanced on the balls of her feet, listening. Timbers creaked around her. A rat squeaked to her left, then scurried from sight. She was alone . . . exactly as she'd hoped.

Silently, graceful as a panther, she padded toward the hold, where the prisoners would be kept.

The hold was but dimly lit. Morgan slipped through the door and took cover behind a barrel of apples, peering out to study the situation. Scully had chained perhaps fifty prisoners here: not just Glasspoole and Blair, but everyone who might have given the slightest thought to supporting her. It had been a purge.

So much the better, she thought. These men had nooses waiting for them in Jamaica; they would have no choice but to follow her . . . a choice between death and freedom wasn't much of a choice.

It took her a few minutes to spot the guards. They were at different ends of the hold, half dozing through their watch. With the prisoners in chains, of course they thought they had nothing to worry about.

She drifted forward like a phantom. Then, in a lightning strike, she covered the man's mouth as she wrenched his head to the side, breaking his neck.

The movement caught the other guard's attention, though. He suddenly leapt to his feet, squinting to see.

Morgan pulled a knife from the dead man's belt and threw it overhanded. With a solid *thunk*, the blade sank hilt-deep into the man's chest. He, too, fell without a sound.

She rose and strode forward. The prisoners began to stir and murmur excitedly among themselves.

"Morgan!" Glasspoole said. "God bless you. I never thought to see you again."

"It's me, Mr. Glasspoole. Shall we take our ship back?"

"Good idea, Captain!" Blair said excitedly.

He grinned—and Glasspoole grinned back at him. A ripple of excitement ran through the hold.

Morgan spotted the keys to the shackles on a peg near the door—far from the prisoners' reach—and quickly fetched them. Kneeling, she released Blair and Glasspoole, and they began releasing all the other men.

"Has anyone seen King Charles?" she asked.

"Nay," Blair said. "We ain't seen naught of him."

"Perhaps he's still in my cabin," she mused. "Now we must take the armory. This way!"

Pausing only to scoop up the first dead man's cutlass, she headed for the ship's armory. On a merchant ship or a naval vessel, weapons were kept strictly guarded to prevent the crews from mutinying or turning pirate; on a pirate ship, though, everyone was armed and the armory was pretty much left open. If you needed a sword, you took one. That was the pirate way.

Morgan pushed the door open, saw the weapons in their racks and unguarded, and gave a quick nod to Blair and Glasspoole. They began pulling out pistols and cutlasses and handing them to everyone present.

"Captain Scully," Tom Scully whispered to himself. He liked the sound of that title. As he stood near the helm, shouting orders as necessary—or even when not necessary—he gloried in the power of his position. Let Black Harry Adams see him now!

"I believe we can ease that mainsheet a foot or so—it'll draw better for it," he called.

"Are you a good swimmer, Mr. Scully?" a very familiar voice said at his shoulder.

A cold wind touched his heart. Scully whirled to find a gun pointed at his chest by Morgan Adams. His gaze swept to the main deck . . . where Morgan's crew held guns and swords on all of his men.

Morgan smiled cruelly. "Let's see, shall we?"

She crossed to the mast, removed Scully's ax, and replaced it with her dagger. Scully swallowed. This, he thought, had to be the worst moment of his life.

* * *

Morgan didn't bother with anything so formal as a plank. She had her men pick up Scully's crew one by one and hurl them overboard, into the sea. Lieutenant Trotter and the other redcoats, holding their hands over their heads, watched under the vigilant eyes of Bowen and a couple of other sailors.

Her men hooted and catcalled, and when Scully himself finally went flying head over heels to splash beside his men, everyone let out a cheer.

"Do you wish a compass, Mr. Scully?" Blair shouted down to him.

"There are islands close by," Morgan called. "I believe you can make them if you swim slowly ... and the sharks don't get you!"

Laughing, she turned and called for more sails, and as her men scampered to obey, the *Morning Star* came about in the wind. Tortuga, she thought—that was the place to celebrate their victory.

Later, after seeing the redcoats chained up and locked away belowdecks, she returned to her cabin. There she paused in the doorway to survey the damage. Surprisingly, Scully had done little to it. Perhaps afraid of Black Harry Morgan's ghost returning to haunt him for it, she thought with a bitter grin.

Her father's old cutlass, hanging on the far wall, caught her eye. She pulled it down, balancing it in her hand. It felt fine ... truly *right*, somehow.

"King Charles!" she called.

A scratching sound came from one of the cabinets. She quickly opened the door—and her monkey leapt out, chittering in delight.

"Well, you've seen what another captain's like," she said jokingly. "Will you take my orders now?"

King Charles saluted smartly, the way she'd taught him, and she grinned back happily.

20

*T*hey seemed to have forgotten him, Shaw thought, but he wasn't sure if that was a good thing.

Sprawled in the hold, next to the treasure chests, he could only watch and sweat as the redcoats wrapped a huge length of chain around all the treasure chests. Even he would have trouble getting at it, Shaw thought. Then Ainslee locked the chain in place with a pair of huge padlocks.

"One for me," Ainslee said, handing a large iron key to Dawg Brown, "and one for you. That should set your mind at ease."

"Trust me," Dawg said, smiling in a winning fashion, "I'm not at all worried."

They headed abovedecks together, passing

not three feet from Shaw. He scarcely glanced at them; what good would it do, after all? With Morgan dead and Trotter and Ainslee both planning to hang him as a pirate, what reason did he have to care?

He was beyond caring, he thought. He was a dead man in all but fact. And nothing could change that now.

Morgan stood on the poopdeck to address her crew. There were only fifty-three men, but they were armed to the teeth and loyal as only her saving their lives could make them.

She took a deep breath, then cut to the heart of the matter: "I'm not one for speeches," she said. "But now is our moment of truth. We can lift away safe but empty-handed, or we can stand up and take back what's ours. You all know Dawg has more men. I say I'd rather have one of you fighting beside me than ten of his. You all know Dawg has greater firepower. I say we have surprise. Thanks to Lieutenant Trotter here, Dawg'll think us friends. We can get alongside him, smash him, and board him before he knows what's happening. You all know Dawg has never been beaten. I say it is our destiny to destroy him. I say we can be sharing our fortune on this very deck before the sun sets this evening."

She looked at her men. They were regarding her seriously.

"The choice is yours," she went on. "I'll not

dispute your decision. I'm no Black Harry Adams, but today I'm your captain, and Harry lives in me. And if you choose to follow me, I swear to you as a shipmate, I'll be the first one aboard the *Reaper*. Who is with me?"

She looked from face to face. Blair, Glasspoole, and Bowen raised their hands at once. Then Tiedmont, then Smith, then Harrison and Glover.

"I am," said first one crewman, then another. "I am!" they cried, "I am!" until finally the whole crew was with her.

Morgan basked in the feel of power. With these men, she thought she could take Port Royal itself.

"Then on!" she cried. "On to the *Reaper*—and our fortunes!"

Three hours later, the redcoats belowdecks had all been relieved of their uniforms with the exception of Lieutenant Trotter. Trotter, an unnatural grin on his face, stood by the wheel, with one of Morgan's men in a redcoat uniform holding a pistol to his back. Several more of Morgan's men, also dressed as redcoats, moved across the deck.

Morgan, Glasspoole, Blair, and Bowen crouched close by, just out of sight of those aboard the *Reaper*.

"Smile, Mr. Trotter, like you was strolling on a Sunday morning," Glasspoole said softly.

Trotter forced a tense, toothy grin. Morgan,

keeping low, turned to eye the *Reaper*'s hull, sliding closer and closer. They would be alongside in ten minutes, Morgan saw. She thought they would be the longest ten minutes of her life.

"We'll edge toward him, Mr. Blair—not so fast as to alarm him."

Dawg raised his spyglass and peered at the *Morning Star*. He spotted Trotter and several of the redcoats standing by the helm. Probably threw Scully in chains, he thought with a low chuckle. That man thought too highly of himself . . . fancied himself a captain, but to Dawg's eye Scully belonged at second mate at best. The ship was running with full sails; Scully showing off, trying to beat them to port, he thought.

He passed the spyglass to Ainslee, who took his turn. "Trotter comes over to speak to us," he said.

Dawg wheeled. "That's interesting," he said.

"He needs advice," Ainslee said. "The fool couldn't tie his shoelaces without instructions. Best let him catch us."

Dawg had his own ideas. "Clew up the topgallants!" he called. Hairs had begun to bristle on his neck, which he always took for a sign of trouble coming. If trouble it was, he'd be ready.

Aboard the *Morning Star*, Morgan pulled out her own spyglass. She saw only her uncle's ship. The British Men-of-War, which had sailed a day ahead of them, were nowhere in sight. She chuckled. The Men-of-War wouldn't be able to help Dawg Brown now.

She looked the *Reaper* over from stem to stern. The crew seemed too busy. Might Dawg suspect something? But how could that be?

"I hope that Mr. Shaw's still alive," Bowen said.

"We've more important things to think of than Mr. Shaw," Morgan said, a little too strongly. But that didn't make it true. Once Bowen said his name—the name she'd been trying to put from her head to concentrate on the task at hand—all her thoughts about him came flooding back unbidden.

He would have died with her.

He would have died *for* her.

But now it was time to fight, she told herself. Keeping low, out of the *Reaper*'s line of sight, she headed forward.

"General quarters, Mr. Snelgrave," Dawg Brown said calmly. A great calm always came over him before a fight; he found it helped him plan and concentrate his energies. "Powder for the guns, but softly, on cat feet."

"What's going on?" Snelgrave asked.

"Just do as I tell you."

"Aye, Captain," Snelgrave said, sounding puzzled, but he hurried off to obey. Dawg nodded once; he wished he had a dozen more like Snelgrave.

To Ainslee he said, "You asked me if I had a favor. Oblige me—since he must hang anyway, let me hang Shaw now."

"This minute?" Ainslee asked. He gave a shrug. "Why not—sooner the better." To a crewman, he said, "Bring Mr. Shaw up and we'll rig for hanging."

The man hurried off. Dawg turned to Reed, who'd been standing to the side making notes in his journal.

"Provide yourself plenty of ink," he said, trying to emulate Ainslee's pompous manner. "This could be one of your best stories."

He sat back and watched while a noose was hung in the rigging. It only took a few minutes. And, just as quickly, Shaw was escorted up to the main deck.

"You've been due this some time, Mr. Shaw," Dawg said, leaning forward to watch his expression. "It's merely been delayed."

Shaw said nothing. Snelgrave shoved him up the shrouds.

Blair passed Morgan the spyglass.

"What is it?" she asked, puzzled.

"You'd best look," he said.

She raised the spyglass to her eye and swept it across the ship. Then she discovered what Blair meant: Shaw being prodded out along the mainyard. A crewman, serving as hangman, slipped a noose around Shaw's neck.

Morgan snatched up a gun, aimed it, and then hesitated.

"Might take out the hangman at this range," Glasspoole said.

" 'Twould be a very lucky shot," Blair said. "Close faster, Morgan?"

Morgan took a deep breath, then glanced down at her crew on the main deck, all of them crouching by their guns. She couldn't do it. She couldn't betray her men.

She lowered the gun. "It would give us away," she said. "He's testing us. Steady as she goes, Mr. Blair."

Dawg continued to watch the hangman tightening the noose around Shaw's neck. The man was moving with deliberate slowness, drawing out the agony, prolonging Shaw's fear and apprehension. Hanging could be a quick death—the body dropped, the rope snapped taut, and the neck broke instantly—or it could be a slow, painful one—lowering the body gently so the neck didn't break and the man's windpipe slowly closed, suffocating him. Dawg Brown had killed well over four hundred men, but hanging had always been special to him. He liked to see it prolonged as much as possible.

"Mr. Snelgrave?" he asked without taking his eyes from Shaw's terrified face. "Are we prepared to fire?"

From the corner of his eye, he saw Snelgrave

turn to his gunner on the maindeck, holding up his arm to commence firing.

Morgan felt the sweat starting to bead on her forehead as she watched Shaw. They were close enough now that she no longer needed the spyglass. The hangman seemed to be tightening the noose with deliberate slowness.

She glanced at the men below her. Every fiber of her being strained to do something—to save Shaw—but she couldn't betray her men. That was the hardest part of being a captain, she realized—caring for those under you more than yourself.

"Sure I can't try it, Captain?" Glasspoole asked from beside her.

Morgan shook her head. She called softly to the gun deck: "Prime your guns!"

Below, she heard the low thunder of cannons rolling as they were hauled up to the closed gun ports. Their gunners, she knew, would be kneeling beside them, burning matches ready in their hands.

The hangman had finished putting the noose around Shaw's neck. He offered Shaw a blindfold, but Shaw declined.

Governor Ainslee's booming voice carried across the water to her, each word sounding like a blow:

"William Shaw," he said, "you have been found guilty of piracy in the province of Jamaica by the authority of the king. The pun-

ishment for piracy is death. I therefore pray
the hangman carry out the sentence—"

Blair suddenly stood and snatched the rifle
from Morgan's hands. She gaped as he turned
and fired in one quick motion.

The hangman plummeted from the *Reaper*'s
rigging.

Morgan wheeled on him. "What the hell are
you doing?" she demanded.

"He's one of us now," Blair said. "We had to
save him."

Morgan didn't know whether to be relieved
or furious. She finally chose relieved.

She leaned over the poop rail, shouting to
the gun crews: "Up ports! Open fire!"

"What in heaven's name?" Ainslee said, gaping
as the hangman fell from the rigging. He hit
the deck with an audible thump.

Dawg felt nothing but delight. He'd guessed
rightly; his instincts hadn't let him down.

"It's Morgan," he said softly, almost to himself. "I knew it! God bless her!" He glanced at
Snelgrave. "Mr. Snelgrave, commence firing!"

21

*C*linging to the yardarm, Shaw watched the battle unfold below him. The gun ports on both ships flew open, and each ship's full battery blasted a broadside into the other. Cannonballs, exploding right and left, sent screaming men flying through the air; decks and railings flew apart like matches. The bitter smell of black powder filled the air, and a haze began to settle over everything.

The *Reaper* staggered from the hits, but the *Morning Star* seemed to take the worst damage. Shaw caught his breath as he saw rigging come crashing down on top of Morgan and several of her men, but she fought her way clear, seemingly uninjured. Half a dozen men were down, maybe more—whether wounded or dead, though, he couldn't tell.

"Fire!" Morgan shouted. "Lively, Mr. Tew! Fast as you can, Mr. Hastings." She turned and shouted to Blair on the poopdeck, "Mr. Blair, close her quickly now!"

Shaw saw the *Morning Star* veer sharply toward the *Reaper*. Both ships fired another salvo, and smoke and flames blasted across the narrowing gap between the two ships.

A cannonball hit the stern, and Shaw saw Dawg fall. A section of the gallery crumbled away to splinters. Shaw felt a moment's elation and would have cheered if it wouldn't have attracted attention to him. He hadn't survived his own hanging to have a pirate turn, spot him, and shoot him straight between the eyes.

More cannonballs exploded across the *Reaper*'s main deck, showering everyone aboard in debris. Suddenly Morgan's men produced pistols and rifles and began firing a heavy barrage into the *Reaper*. Many of Dawg's men fell, screaming, and panic suddenly rippled through the crew. Morgan had definitely gotten the better part of that one, he thought with satisfaction.

Shaw couldn't help himself. "Get 'em, Morgan!" he yelled. "Show 'em what you're made of!"

"Bastard!" one of Dawg's men growled up at Shaw. "I will slit one throat today, if it be the last thing I do!" He began to climb into the rigging.

Shaw gulped, looked around for a way to defend himself, saw none, and in desperation began to climb. When he glanced down, Dawg's men was gaining on him, a long and very sharp looking knife clenched in his teeth.

Morgan felt fire surging through her veins. This was Dawg's last day on earth. She'd seen him fall, and as she stalked across the deck, sword in hand, shouting commands and encouragement to her men, she knew this was meant to be the greatest triumph of her life.

"Hoist our colors!" she called.

One of the crewmen produced the Jolly Roger and ran it to the mizzen top. As the flag unfurled, showing a skull and crossbones, Morgan shouted to the fiddler and a drummer beside him: *"Play!"*

They started up a martial theme that slowly sped up with each refrain. It would keep the men moving, she thought, and it would help strike terror into those they were fighting. It showed she was confident of victory.

To the gunner, she said, "Pour it into him!"

"Fire!" the gunner called, and another barrage crossed the twenty yards now separating the two ships. Dawg lost one cannon and at least a dozen redcoats, Morgan saw with satisfaction. She was ripping him to shreds.

Eighteen yards ... fifteen ...

* * *

Dawg clawed his way free of the wreckage, cutlass clenched in one fist. His face was flushed, and he felt blood trickling from half a dozen minor wounds, but he brushed it all away and tried to concentrate.

Morgan's ship was growing closer. They were going to try to board him, he thought with amazement. They were losing the fight and they were going to board *him*. Had she lost her mind?

"Fire!" he screamed. "Blast them from the sea! They want your treasure—will you let them take it?"

His men held their positions and began prepping the cannons to fire. On his gunner's command, a new salvo raked across the *Morning Star* ... and one lucky shot hit the poopdeck, knocking Morgan off her feet, but she picked herself up immediately, unhurt. Dawg felt a pang of disappointment. It might have been interesting if she'd lost a limb or an eye.

Fully half the cannonballs missed their targets, though, and went splashing into the sea. Damn them ... his men were panicked. He'd have to force them back in line.

"Point her up!" he heard Morgan calling over the noise of small-arms fire. "Riflemen forward! Boarders, prepare!"

Dawg stalked forward through the smoke

and confusion. "Where are my muskets? *Where are my muskets?*"

Ten yards . . . eight . . .

Morgan felt her heart beginning to pound. The *Morning Star* was closing with the *Reaper*. Dawg's men were climbing to the forecastle and opening fire; she and her men ducked the shots.

Blair yelled up to her, "He makes to board us first!"

"We'll have to take them first!" She turned to her marksmen. "Give them a volley—fire!"

Her men took aim and fired in unison. The shots ripped through Dawg's men, but those who fell were just as quickly replaced by others. Dawg had not only the redcoats aboard, but his full crew, Morgan thought, and he outmanned her two-to-one in the best of times. Now, with only fifty-three men, it was more like five-to-one.

She heard Dawg cry, "Fire! Knock them down!"

The return fire decimated Morgan's twenty-odd riflemen. But it was too late to worry—the ships were only feet apart.

A rain of grappling hooks flew from the *Reaper*. Some missed and fell toward the water, but more still took hold. A few caught men and pierced them; others held tightly on rails and rigging. The grapplers aboard the *Reaper* heaved on their lines, pulling the two ships together. Fast as her men cut down a grappler, though, another rose to take his place.

The two ships crunched together with a jolt that threw Morgan and everyone else off their feet. She leapt back up.

"Boarders away!" Dawg called.

"Keep firing!" Morgan said. "Hold them back!"

Hand over hand or on ropes, Dawg's men swung across onto the *Morning Star*'s deck. Morgan's men rushed to repel them, and the battle began to break down into little knots of fighting.

Morgan found herself facing three of Dawg's men. She pulled her pistol and shot the first one in the chest, threw her gun at another, who ducked, and ran the third through with her cutlass when he watched the flying pistol rather than her. Wrenching the blade free, she turned and attacked the remaining man, raining a staggering series of blows on him.

Feinting, she caught him off guard and clobbered him across the side of his head with her sword. When he fell, she slit his throat, then waded into the fray, slashing, stabbing, trying to rally her men to victory.

Shaw had raced toward the top of the mast with a pirate on his heels. He prayed Morgan would notice and somehow shoot the blackguard, but she was too busy to even notice him now, he quickly realized.

He reached a yardarm and crawled out across the sail. Perhaps he could somehow climb or slide down, he thought.

Two feet below him, the pirate paused, pulled the knife from his teeth, and tried to slash Shaw's leg. Yelping in fear, Shaw jerked his leg out of the way, then allowed his weight to swing him back. He gave the man a kick to the side of the head.

Grinning, the pirate shook it off and advanced on him again.

A cannon shot suddenly blasted the yardarm right behind the pirate, and the two of them plummeted toward the deck. Then the sail caught in the rigging, forming a sort of net, and Shaw tumbled into it. The pirate, screaming, his face contorted with rage, fell past and hit the deck with a thump.

Shaw caught his breath for a few heartbeats, then rolled over, grabbed a rope, and began to climb down. Suddenly the rigging didn't seem the safest place to be anymore.

He dropped the last six feet to the deck, saw a dead pirate with a cutlass in his hand, and pried the weapon from the man's grip. Armed, able to defend himself for the first time, he tried to draw back—perhaps he could find a place to hide till the battle was over—when several more of Dawg's men spotted him.

They charged, and he turned and ran toward the foredeck. There, at least, only one or two would be able to get at him at a time. Thank goodness he knew how to use a sword. He'd never liked fighting, but pressed hard and with his life at stake, he had no doubt he'd hold his own . . . or die trying.

He'd killed three and was beginning to beat off his last attacker when the two ships came together. The pirate he'd been facing—a tall, broad-shouldered man whose arms and bare chest were covered with tattoos of ships and mermaids—slammed hard to the deck, and Shaw fell on top of him.

He hammered the man's head with the pommel of his sword, then leapt to his feet. Slowly, groggily, the man rose. He'd dropped his cutlass and seemed confused.

There was a gap in the railing. Shaw gave himself a running start, then shoved the man through the hole and into the ocean. He fell without a sound, hit the water, and sank with barely a ripple.

Breathing hard, Shaw sat on the forecastle's steps to try to catch his breath. Then he pulled himself to his feet. The battle had moved aboard the *Morning Star*. Morgan needed him.

He started across, grimly determined to save the woman he loved.

Belowdecks, Reed had been making careful notes in his journal when the battle started. The explosions jolted him, knocking him from side to side, spilling his ink.

He picked himself up, gathered his pouch

and journal, and headed topside. His first real battle, he thought with growing excitement. What a story *this* would make!

When he emerged onto the deck, the stillness of everything shocked him. Bodies lay everywhere, and blood and broken rigging covered the deck. A hazy cloud of black smoke, acrid and unpleasant, hovered around him.

Slowly he moved forward until he could see what was going on aboard the *Morning Star.*

The ship's decks ran with blood. Everyone was covered in red. As he watched, a man not fifteen feet from him lost an arm and fell, screaming, clutching the stump, only to be run through by a sword.

He swallowed, sick inside. "My God," he whispered. "My God."

The battle was lost. Morgan realized it the moment wave after wave of Dawg's men boarded her ship. Sheer numbers alone would drive them down.

She did her best, striding through the battle, lending a hand here, stabbing there, killing more than a dozen of Dawg's men. But it wasn't enough. There always seemed to be five or ten more waiting to press their attack.

Slowly her men began to rally around her, many injured but all still fighting. This would be a fight to the death, she realized. There could be no quarter; falling prisoner meant death.

"There are too many of them!" Glasspoole said, fighting beside her.

"Keep fighting," she told him. "Hold them as long as you can." She finished her man off, then turned and headed toward the *Reaper*.

"Where are you going?" Glasspoole asked, finishing his man as well.

"To blow out his bottom and get what we came for. Cut us loose when I do."

She grabbed a line and swung across the *Reaper*'s deck.

22

*S*haw had almost reached the *Morning Star* when a familiar figure came striding toward him out of the smoke. It was Governor Ainslee, sword in hand, a savage grin etched across his mouth. He had blood on his arms and chest—and somehow Shaw knew it wasn't the governor's own.

"Mr. Shaw," Ainslee said, "I believe you're the cause of all this."

He charged suddenly, and Shaw gave ground before him. He parried Ainslee's first cut, then parried again and again as the governor launched a blistering attack. Forced to retreat step by step, Shaw found himself driven up onto the bowsprit, directly over the skeleton figurehead.

Still Ainslee pressed his attack, thrusting, feinting, thrusting again. Shaw was knocked off balance, teetered, and then fell.

He managed to catch hold of the skeleton figurehead and found himself dangling above the water. Looking up, he found the governor smiling with satisfaction.

"And so the story ends, Mr. Shaw," Ainslee said. "You've run out of tricks."

"Can't hear you, m'lord—" Shaw called. "Bend a bit closer . . ."

Ainslee slashed downward at Shaw's hands, but Shaw moved faster. Pulling himself around the figurehead and up the other side, he came up behind Ainslee—and as Ainslee whirled, Shaw ran him through.

The governor's eyes widened as he stared down at his chest. He tipped backward toward the sea. Shaw reached out the moment before Ainslee fell and snatched the key from around his neck.

Ainslee screamed, then vanished beneath the ship's bow as the ocean took him.

And now, Shaw thought, hefting the key, *to get the treasure.* If they'd hang him as a pirate, he'd be the best pirate he could. And he knew, somehow, that taking the treasure— even if all he did was to dump it overboard— would be the greatest blow against Dawg that he could make. He'd have to trust to Morgan's skill with sword and pistol to carry the battle.

* * *

Dawg's men followed Morgan back aboard the *Reaper*. She cut a swath through them, slashing, thrusting, parrying, always pressing forward. By God, she'd kill them all if she had to!

Suddenly she found herself face-to-face with John Reed.

"Morgan," he said, ashen-faced, "I betrayed you, but that's what love does. Can you ever find it in yourself to forgive me?"

Morgan opened her mouth to reply, but before she could, a pirate swung down from the rigging, a pistol in his hand. He was aiming for her, but Reed threw himself in the way—and the pirate shot him instead.

Morgan didn't hesitate. She killed the pirate before he could defend himself, then lingered a moment over her former friend. He had betrayed her. She'd known it deep inside, but she had not wanted to face the awful truth.

There was nothing more she could say or do, except perhaps say a prayer for him later and give him an honorable burial at sea, if she survived that long.

Turning, she leapt off the poopdeck onto the main deck. She'd need a cannon to hole the *Reaper*, and the only place she'd find one of those was the gun deck.

She went down a hatch cautiously, then made her way forward. Most of Dawg's crewmen here were dead, their cannons upended. The surviving gunners had joined the attack on her ship, she knew. She spotted a stack of powder barrels and another of larger powder tubs. That should do the trick nicely.

Kicking one of the barrels over, she rolled it toward the tubs, leaving a trail of black powder from the open spout. Then, leaving it there, she picked up one of the still-burning slow matches used to set off cannon charges, touched it into the trail, and leapt back as the powder ignited with a *whoosh*.

She dove for cover as flames raced toward the powder tubs.

As Shaw was making his way to the treasure chests, the deck in front of him suddenly exploded in fire, smoke, and a geyser of water. The blast threw him from his feet, and suddenly broken bits of wood began raining down on him. He covered his head. What had happened? Had the *Morning Star* fired a cannon at him?

When he looked up, the rigging had caught fire, and one by one the sails blossomed into flame. The whole ship was starting to burn.

Shouts of "She's sinking!" and "Abandon ship!" came from Dawg's men still aboard. Some raced to try to put out the fire; others fled for the safety of the *Morning Star*.

Shaw knew he had to move quickly. The ship did seem to be settling lower in the water—and between that and the flames, he had little hope of the *Reaper's* lasting much longer.

Clutching his key, he ran for the treasure. Even if he could save only one chest—

Blair glared defiantly at Bishop. Dawg's men had cut him, and cut him badly, and pain racked the whole side of his body, but he had no intention of lying down and dying meekly. By sheer force of will he remained on his feet, holding his cutlass out before him . . . only a little bit shaky.

"Time to beg," Bishop said. He struck Blair's sword and sent it flying. "A quick death, Mr. Blair, or a slow, painful one with a wound to the guts?"

Blair caught movement from the corner of his eye—someone racing to help. Mr. Bowen—

"An English officer asked me that same question," he began, trying to draw out the conversation. "I told him what I now tell you. Simply this. The good God put me on this Earth, and that was for a reason. If it is to die at your hand, then it's not a question of mercy, but of truth."

"Truth?" Bishop said, furrows growing in his brow. "What the hell is that supposed to mean?"

Bowen, racing up, stabbed Bishop in the hip. Bishop gave a scream and fell, and Blair fell on him. He pinned Bishop's arms with his knees and tightened his hands around Bishop's throat.

"Thanks, Mr. Bowen!" he called, but Bowen seemed to have vanished.

Only when Bishop's eyes stuck out and his tongue turned black did Blair roll off him. Killing Bishop had given him new strength, he thought.

Snatching up his sword, he strode more confidently into the fight.

Glasspoole tightened his grip on his sword as Snelgrave advanced on him, whirling his chain over his head so fast it made a whistling sound. He didn't know what to watch: that deadly length of chain or the cutlass in Snelgrave's one good hand.

He retreated slowly but steadily, crossing the deck, looking desperately for something—anything—that could help.

Snelgrave whipped the chain at him, and he danced back, swinging savagely with his sword. Sparks flew as steel met rusted iron, and Glasspoole felt the blow through the whole length of his arm. His hand began to grow numb.

Grinning, Snelgrave continued his advance. Slowly he began to swing the chain again.

They had reached the anchor. Glasspoole deliberately left his right side open, and as Snelgrave whipped back his arm for a killing blow, the chain wrapped around the anchor's wooden crossbeams ... exactly as Glasspoole had wanted.

He leapt forward, slashed the anchor keeper, and the anchor dropped overboard, yanking Snelgrave with it. He had a startled, disbelieving look on his face. The anchor hit the water with a loud splash, carrying the pirate to a watery grave.

Glasspoole wiped sweat from his brow. Then Blair reached him.

"Time to rally the men, Mr. Glasspoole," he said.

"Aye," Glasspoole said. Morgan needed them. They couldn't let her down.

Taking a deep breath, he shouted, "Morgan's won the day! Rally around me and we'll push Dawg's bastards into the deep!"

Men began taking up the shout—"Morgan's won the day! Morgan's won the day!"—and drawing new strength, Morgan's men attacked furiously. They used pistols and rifles and belaying pins as clubs; they used marlinespikes, swords, and knives; they used any weapon that came to hand.

And Dawg's men—hearing that they were beaten—seemed to give up some of their strength. They fell back everywhere under the fierce counterattack.

"Now it's our turn!" Glasspoole shouted, running one of Dawg's men through, then ripping his cutlass free. "Pour it into them! You, forward—cut us loose!"

Men at the front of the ship began to sever the grappling lines. Even with so few sails still full, there would be more than enough wind to pull away from the burning *Reaper*, Glasspoole thought. Morgan had done it. Treasure or no treasure, she'd beaten Dawg's men.

Belowdecks, the *Reaper* had begun to fill with water. Shaw had reached the hold where Ainslee had chained up the treasure chests. He fitted Ainslee's key into the first lock, turned, and heard a satisfyingly loud snap as it popped open. Then he tried the key in the second padlock, and though it fit into the hole, it wouldn't turn.

Damn him, he thought. Why couldn't Ainslee have been trying to cheat Dawg? Why couldn't the governor's key fit both locks?

An explosion sounded, rocking the ship. The chests shifted as the ship began to list to the side. Suddenly they gave way, rumbling across the floor toward him. Shaw tried to push them out of the way, but they were too heavy and just kept coming, forcing him back.

Suddenly he found his back against the bulkhead. The chests slid forward and pinned him. He shoved at them, but they wouldn't budge—he was trapped.

"Hey!" he shouted. "Help! Anyone! I'm

trapped down here!" He continued to struggle to free himself.

"Mr. Shaw," he heard Dawg's voice calling from somewhere close by. "The wicked little fly in my ointment. Come to seek my treasure, I presume?"

Shaw looked around, but didn't spot Dawg. Hearing a low chuckle, he looked up. Dawg stood overhead, next to the hold's open hatch, gazing down at him. Flames filled the sails behind him. Despite his words and smile, he did not appear at all amused.

"Don't move," Dawg said. "I'll be right down."

Morgan had spotted Dawg on her way back to her ship. She veered toward him at once and heard every word he said to William Shaw.

"No, you won't," she told him.

Dawg looked up at her and his faintly mocking smile spread into an outright grin. This must have been what he was waiting for, Morgan thought. As it was what she had been waiting for. She had a lot of old scores to settle with her uncle, and this was the time to do it.

"Morgan, run, don't fight!" Shaw urged her from below. "If she burns down to her powder, she'll blow to smithereens."

Morgan ignored him. She hefted her cutlass as Dawg came around the hold hatch toward her, passing through flames and stepping over corpses.

"He don't understand us," Dawg said softly, "does he? Not for one minute. But then, he's not family."

He attacked suddenly, his sword a stinging blur, thrusting and probing at all her defenses. Morgan had to give ground. She couldn't stand up to his onslaught. He was overpowering her with sheer muscle.

Then Dawg's foot caught for a second in a loop of rope from the fallen rigging, and he staggered a bit, off balance. Morgan saw her chance and attacked, driving him back in turn with a tremendous flurry of cuts and thrusts. For the first time, Dawg began to look concerned, and he retreated warily before her.

"Just you and me now, Dawg."

"I see you're in a hurry to join your father," he spat back.

"He had no sword, Dawg—it's your preference. I, on the other hand, do . . ."

"Your death will just be slower!"

He parried and counter-thrust suddenly, and Morgan danced back easily, leaping into the shrouds and clambering toward the main topsail. She knew he was a lot stronger than she was, and though they seemed well matched as swordsmen, he could tire her out, then finish her at his leisure. She had to change tactics, force him to fight on her terms, and she thought that bringing the fight into the air—where agility mattered more than strength—just might do the trick.

When she glanced down, Dawg was following right on her heels.

23

The last of Dawg's men were rapidly being subdued aboard the *Morning Star*. Blair, clutching his hand to his side to try to stanch the flow of blood from Bishop's wound, leaned against the rail.

"Where's the captain?" he heard Bowen shout.

"Still aboard the *Reaper*," Glasspoole shouted back.

Blair whirled to see—and spotted Morgan and Dawg fighting in the rigging of the burning ship. His made a fist and pounded the railing with it. There was nothing he could do to help.

Morgan dodged around the mast as Dawg swung for her. His blade hit a chunk of wood from the mast, but he wrenched it free before she could gain any advantage. He parried her quick ripostes—then, holding on to a rope with one hand, she kicked him in the chest. He looked surprised.

"That was for Mordechai," Morgan said. "The next one will be for Harry."

She pressed him hard, sword clanging on sword, and she pushed him back. For a second she thought she had him, but then he rallied and began to force her back farther up the shrouds into the rigging.

As she climbed higher, Morgan looked down and saw the whole ship burning below them. The heat on her face was terrible.

"Your father was nothing," Dawg told her. "You exceed him. Think what we could do together. The two of us, your ship, mine—the world would tremble. You don't have to die."

"You do!" Morgan snarled back. She couldn't let him distract her. He'd murdered her father and two of her uncles, and he'd tried to murder her. Revenge was the only thing that mattered.

She thrust, and he parried—and gave his wrist a twist that knocked her cutlass away. She leapt to a buntline before he could run her through, trying to pull herself up to the topsail.

"You've run out of world, niece!" Dawg called after her.

He slashed the buntline in two, and Morgan

fell. She passed the boom, screaming, and smashed bodily through the grating on the main deck and down onto the gun deck below.

It left her dazed and shaken, and she had a sharp pain in her left shoulder and ribs. Slowly, painfully, she sat up. She looked around desperately—and spotted Shaw trapped behind the treasure.

"Morgan, damn you," he said. "Clear out while you can!"

"Not while Dawg still breathes!"

"A noble sentiment," Dawg replied from overhead. He slowly descended the ladder to the gun deck, and Morgan had the impression he was savoring the moment. "The odd thing is, Morgan, I enjoyed it—I'm sorry it's over. What else will I now have to sustain me—why else will I get up in the morning?"

Morgan scrambled back from the ladder. He followed.

"I'm sure," Dawg went on, "I'll find something to occupy me. Do give my best to Harry when you see him."

He raised his cutlass. Morgan looked around frantically, hoping to find an abandoned weapon. The only thing at hand was a burning stick that had fallen in from the deck.

She snatched it up and pointed it toward him. Dawg smiled.

"It's over, niece," he said softly, "or are you planning to fight me with that stick?"

"No, uncle," she said. "With *this*."

She whipped away a length of sail canvas, revealing a cannon. She'd thought she recognized its outline. Since the muzzle hadn't been pointing up, she figured it had to be loaded.

She thrust the burning stick to the touchhole.

"Bad Dawg," she told him.

And then the cannon fired.

Dawg's body was blasted out the ship's stern galleries and into the ocean, leaving a bloody pink smear over everything along the way.

Morgan didn't have time to gloat. The *Reaper* was listing more than before, and the corner where Shaw sat pinned in by treasure had begun to fill with water. She splashed out to try to help.

Shaw's head was underwater, but she could see him struggling. Throwing her strength in with his, she found they still couldn't budge the treasure chests.

Shaw was starting to drown, arms flailing. Grabbing a cannon swab, Morgan took a deep breath and dove down, using the long pole to try to lever him free.

At last the chests shifted, freeing his leg. Seizing his shirt, she pulled him up toward the surface, then dragged him to a dry part of the deck.

He was unconscious. She pressed her lips against his, breathing her breath into him. His eyes opened slowly, and then she saw recognition and joy in his eyes . . . and she knew it mirrored her own expression. They kissed. The water was almost up to the overhead, with only six inches to go, but she didn't care. She loved him, and that was all the world.

"Bless me," Shaw said, "I believe I've died and gone to heaven."

"Little chance they'd let you in, William. Shall we go?"

"You're forgetting something," he said.

"Not bloody likely."

They looked at each other and grinned, and then as one they dove into the water. Shaw reached the chests just ahead of her and tried to budge them, but Morgan already knew that was hopeless. Instead, she swam toward a rope and a barrel and began tying them together. This was their only hope, she thought.

When her lungs began to burn for air, she had to let go, though, and surface. She popped up beside Shaw, in a little pocket of air. They had only inches in which to breathe and talk.

"Can't budge it an inch," Shaw said.

"And we never will," she said. "Best get out while we can."

He nodded, then swam toward the ladder leading through the hatch. Morgan took another deep breath, then dove back toward the barrel and the rope. She had just one more thing to finish . . .

The two ships were about ten feet apart when Shaw gained the deck. He looked back for Morgan, but she hadn't followed yet. Probably making one last try for the treasure, he thought—she could be very stubborn when money was involved, he knew.

She'd be along as fast as she could. He waited on the rail, staring back toward the hold, wondering if he should fetch her—or if that would only annoy her.

Finally she climbed out of the hold, looking tired and drained. He held out his hand, and when she took it, he swung her up onto the rail beside him. Together, they leapt toward the *Morning Star.*

Behind them, the ship exploded as fire reached the powder stores.

"The captain—" Blair said. The explosion had thrown him off his feet.

Now, turning, he stared into a cloud of black smoke. Bits of wreckage floated in and out of sight, some still burning. The *Reaper* had been reduced to kindling wood. He didn't see how anyone could have lived through the explosion.

"The captain—" he said again. The words caught in his throat. He'd come to love her like his own daughter.

Glasspoole shook his head slowly. "I don't see her."

"We'll search," Blair said. "There must be something left of them to bury."

The smoke began to clear, but Shaw still heard a ringing sound in his ears. He clung to a piece of wreckage with Morgan. Only slowly did he realize it was the skeleton figurehead.

"We made it, sweet Morgan," he said. "I'm afraid, however, the treasure lies far beneath us."

"Maybe something will turn up."

"Drag the ocean with hooks? Send down a magnet? It don't matter. Listen to me—I've never said anything like this in all my life. I don't care. I have you—there will be other treasures."

Just then there was a tremendous upswelling near by, and a barrel breached the surface beside them.

"This one will do," Morgan said.

"It's just a barrel—"

Morgan gave him a knowing look and swam over to it. She touched the rope tied around the barrel's middle and seemed to find it satisfactory.

"And this is just a rope," she told him. "But on the end—"

Shaw didn't know what to say. Morgan—and the treasure, too. It seemed almost too good to be true.

He beamed at her.

24

A mosaic of diamonds, rubies, and gold. Jeweled daggers, crucifixes, and goblets. Coins, necklaces, and rings. It was an almost unimaginable fortune, exceeding her wildest dreams and expectations.

The crew had assembled around the pile of treasure which now occupied the center of the maindeck. Morgan smiled and glanced over at Shaw, who stood beside her on the poopdeck.

"This is yours, lads," she called down to her men. "Every last doubloon. No one ever fought harder for anything."

They just stared at the fortune before them, transfixed. Morgan found she didn't blame them. It was more than any of them had ever seen before.

"Mr. Glasspoole will divide it into equal shares," she went on. She moved forward to the edge of the rail. "You're all rich men now, and you're free to go your separate ways." She grinned. "You could buy a little cottage in Bermuda and sip camomile tea on the porch." She snickered at her own joke, but she seemed to be the only one.

She went on, "On the other hand, we could do what we're born to do: stick together and ride the early Trades all the way to Madagascar or India, loaded with booty and no navy for a thousand miles."

She paused a moment to let her words sink in.

"Well?" she demanded. "What do you say? Do we add to this pile here on the deck?" She pointed to the treasure expectantly.

Nobody replied. She turned to Glasspoole.

"Mr. Glasspoole? What say you?"

He didn't meet her gaze. "Aye . . ." he said. "But it's such a big decision to make in such a little while . . ."

Morgan felt her eyes widen in surprise. She turned to Blair.

"Mr. Blair?" she demanded.

He hemmed and hawed for a second, then said, "I'd like to—it's just that I always wanted to do a bit of farming . . ."

Morgan stared in disbelief. *"Farming!"* she exclaimed.

"I know it sounds silly," Blair said.

"It sounds great," Bowen said.

Morgan whirled to face Shaw. "Mr. Shaw, what do you say?"

Their eyes locked. They were inches from each other, and Morgan realized their moment of truth had come. Shaw smiled a very charming smile.

"Well . . ." he began. "It's just that . . . we do have so much . . . and Madagascar is so far away . . ."

Another man called, "And it would be hard to serve under someone who doesn't even have a sword."

"What?" Morgan said, looking around in confusion.

"On the other hand," Shaw said, starting to smile, "if she had a fine cutlass like this one . . ."

He produced a beautiful jewel-handled cutlass. Morgan stared down at the emeralds and rubies set into the hilt. The gold filigree gleamed in the sunlight. Holding it out to her, he smiled again.

Glasspoole said, "Now that's more fitting of a *captain.*"

Shaw put the sword in Morgan's hand as she stared down at it. After a heartbeat, the entire crew broke into uproarious laughter around the deck.

It was a joke, Morgan realized, suddenly understanding. "You blaggards . . ." she said sheepishly.

"With a sword like that," Blair said, "I'd follow my captain anywhere."

More laughter rang out. Morgan looked down at the blade, admiring it.

Bowen said, "We found it at the bottom of the chest. It was your grandfather's."

"His name is engraved right there on the blade," Shaw added.

She tilted it toward the sun and watched the light catch on the ornate lettering: HARRY.

"To the captain!" another of her men called, and she looked up from the sword to a rousing cheer.

"To the captain!" the whole crew cried, raising their swords.

"Where to, Morgan?" Shaw asked.

"I told you," Morgan said. "Madagascar."

"But that's in *Africa*," he said.

"Then we best get busy. Mr. Taskar, take the crow's nest watch for the next twelve hours."

"Good as done, ma'am, captain," Taskar said.

"Mr. Blair," Morgan went on, "prepare to come about bearing South Southeast: one three zero." She paused and glanced over at Shaw. "And Mr. Shaw—I'd like to see you in my cabin. Immediately."

The crew snapped-to as the *Morning Star*

began to turn about on her new heading. Morgan watched them for a moment, all the cogs moving together like a finely oiled machine. Then she gave Shaw a sly smile and moved past him down the stairs toward her cabin.

He grinned and followed.